The Toilet of Doom

ORCHARD BOOKS

First published in Great Britain in 2001 by Orchard Books
This edition first published in 2014 by Orchard Books
This edition published in 2017 by The Watts Publishing Group

3 5 7 9 10 8 6 4 2

Text copyright © Michael Lawrence, 2001
Illustrations copyright © Donough O'Malley, 2014

The moral rights of the author and illustrator have been asserted.

A CIP catalogue record for this book
is available from the British Library.

ISBN 978 1 40832 424 0

Printed and bound in Great Britain by
Clays Ltd, St Ives plc

The paper and board used in this book are
made from wood from responsible sources.

Orchard Books
An imprint of
Hachette Children's Group
Part of The Watts Publishing Group Limited
Carmelite House
50 Victoria Embankment
London EC4Y 0DZ

An Hachette UK Company
www.hachette.co.uk

www.hachettechildrens.co.uk

MICHAEL LAWRENCE

ORCHARD

chapter one

ever had the feeling that your life's been flushed down the toilet? I have. And it wasn't just a feeling. I knew something was wrong the moment I woke up that Sunday morning. But before I get to the Big Flush I'd better fill you in on how it all started.

It was the previous Friday – another day I woke up feeling that something wasn't right. This time it was my nose. I rolled out of bed and plodded to the bathroom, where the mirror over the basin informed me that there was a lump on my hooter the size of a satellite dish. I sighed, imagining the day's pathetic jokes at my expense, and left the bathroom.

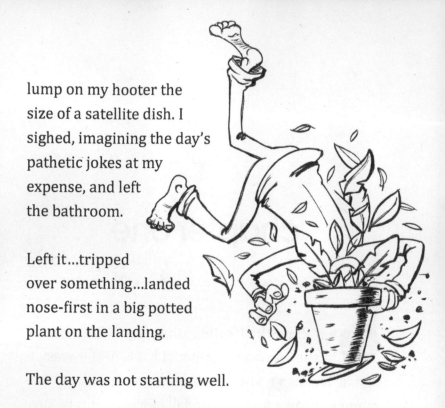

Left it...tripped over something...landed nose-first in a big potted plant on the landing.

The day was not starting well.

I pulled my face out of the leaves to see what had tripped me. Stallone, our cat, lay across the doorway like a draught excluder. He must have seen me go into the bathroom and thrown himself across the door to catch me on the way out. Never misses a chance to trip me, that cat. Me or Dad. Never trips Mum. He's nice as pie to her. Any female actually. My mother says he's a woman's cat. Dad says they're welcome to him.

'You did that on purpose,' I said. 'You...*animal*.'

Stallone stared back at me with those mean green eyes of his as if to say, 'Wanna make something of it, pal?'

The worst of it was the potted plant. It had only been there since yesterday and suddenly, day two, half its leaves and earth were on the carpet. Mum would go berserk. I got up and raced to my room.

I rummaged under the bed, found what I was looking for. At last I had a good use for my Maths exercise book! While I was down there I grabbed the ball of chewing gum I'd been building up piece by piece for months. I licked the fluff off and jammed it in my mouth to soften it. It tasted like the inside of a fisherman's boot, but I wasn't rearing it for a taste contest. Another couple of months and my gumball would have been big enough to break some

sort of record. Would have. If Stallone hadn't made me use it to stick leaves back on a potted plant.

I was on my knees scooping earth back in the pot with my trusty Maths book when Dad strolled along the landing in his boxer shorts and "***I'm not old, I'm a recycled teenager***" T-shirt.

'What happened?'

I took the softened gumball out of my mouth.

'Tripped over cat, fell in plant.'

'Your mum'll crucify you.'

'Only if we have a snitch in the family,' I said, starting on the leaves.

'Leaves fell off, did they?' he asked.

'Yeah. Sticking 'em back with chewing gum.'

'Good move. Just what I'd have done.'

'When you were a kid, you mean?'

'I mean now. You know what the old girl's like with her rotten plants.' He noticed Stallone sprawling across the bathroom door and raised his foot. 'Gertcha!'

Stallone got up, glaring at him with real hatred, and slunk off lashing his tail like a whip.

'Jiggy, are you up yet?'

My mother's voice from downstairs. Dad shot into the bathroom and bolted the door. I looked down. Mum stood at the bottom of the stairs in her dressing gown, glaring up at me like I'd committed some crime. I had – the potted plant – but she didn't know that. Yet.

'On my way,' I said. She started up the stairs. Panic. There were still some leaves on the floor, and quite a bit of earth. 'I said I'm on my **way**!'

'And I'm coming up to get dressed, d'you mind?' she said.

I grabbed the leaves, crammed them in my mouth – useful things, mouths – chewed like a starving cow, swallowed hard. Then I scooped up the earth and dropped it in my pyjama trousers. It would have helped if I'd been wearing bicycle clips, but you don't usually get those with pyjamas.

I headed downstairs, casually rubbing my nose.

'You'll be late,' Mum snapped, coming up.

'And good morning to you too,' I said, going down.

We drew near. It was going to be a close thing. Half the garden was trickling down my legs. My knees couldn't keep it off the ground for ever. But of course Mum stopped. Squinted at me.

'What's that on your nose? Looks like earth.'

'Earth?' I said. 'Well thanks very much. I mean I know it's big, but I didn't think it was the size of a *planet*.'

I carried on down, with no idea that the thing on my nose was going to be the one bright spot of my day. Next six days actually. By this time next week I would have been to hell and back.

Twice.

chapter two

after breakfast I got dressed in time to be almost late for school, as usual. Then I crossed the road to Pete and Angie's.

Pete and Angie are my oldest buds. They're not related to one another, but they live in the same house these days, along with his dad and her mum. We call ourselves The Three Musketeers (the kids, not the parents) and we have this Musketeery slogan,

'One for all and all for lunch!'

which we cry whenever we leap into action, which is a bit too often for my liking.

They came out seconds before I got to the door. We have this almost-late business down to a fine art. And of course, true to form, the first thing Pete said was: 'I like the nose, did you pick it yourself?'

I ignored him. Best thing to do with Pete most of the time. But Angie was looking too. You don't ignore Angie Mint. Not if you want to live.

'OK,' I said. 'Get it out of your system.'

'Get what out of my system?'

'The stupid remark about my conk.'

She looked offended. 'I'm offended,' she said.

'You are?' I said. 'Oh. Sorry.'

'I should think so. I would never be so unkind as to make fun of a face that's been taken over by a giant plum tomato that probably glows in the dark.'

'Thanks, Ange.'

We set off for school.

'Oi, wait for me!'

We groaned. Eejit Atkins. Ralph to his mum, the teachers and social workers, Eejit to his dad and everyone else.

'We'll never get this right,' Angie muttered.

What she meant was that ever since Eejit moved in next door to me we've been trying to get to school without him and we usually don't make it. It's like he waits for us behind the Atkins family wheely

bin and shoots out the
moment we appear.

Eejit fell in step
beside me and
chattered like a
chipmunk halfway to
school while we three talked
among ourselves. But then he
caught sight of a couple of his
Neanderthal pals loping along the
opposite pavement and zigzagged across the road
to join them.

We reached school just in time for the bell, and
headed for Registration.

Friday mornings aren't too bad at Ranting Lane
School, but the afternoons are a real snoozefest.
This is because the last two lessons of the week
are RE with Mr Prior and Maths with Mr Dakin. Mr
Prior (Old Priory) isn't a strong man. Kids make
him twitch. He'd been off all week having a nervous
breakdown at his mother's, which meant that other

teachers had been standing in for him. And who did we get that Friday? Dakin.

Now Face-Ache Dakin is nobody's favourite. Besides being our miserable Maths teacher he's  our miserable form tutor, which means that we see more of him than just about any other life-form on Earth. Even his son Milo doesn't like him much. Milo's in our class, and while his old man is Mr Grim, Mr Strict, Milo is one of the nicest kids there. Now that he was in charge of both last lessons Dakin Senior decided to change the order of them, Maths first, RE last.

When the time came to switch to RE, Dakin called three of us out and pointed to a small brown suitcase he'd brought in with him.

'Open that,' he told them, 'divide up what you find inside, and place a copy on every desk.'

We all threw our necks up on poles to see what was in the case, then took them off the poles when we saw. Books. Old books with black covers. The class erupted in groans.

'Yes, class,' Dakin said:
'Bibles. King James's Bibles.'

'Won't he miss them, sir?'
I said.

'The Bibles you are used to,' he went on, 'are modern mass-market translations. The language in them is dull, flat, uninspiring. These, on the other hand...' He stroked the cover of the one on his desk. 'You are about to have an experience denied most of today's children. You are going to hear the words of the Bible as they should be heard. Speak them as they should be spoken.'

I tipped my chair back and spoke over my shoulder to Milo.

'What's the old loon up to, Milo?'

'He's been longing for a chance to show these off,' Milo said. 'They used to be in my Aunt Trixie's religious bookshop. They've been under the bed in our spare room ever since it was turned into a Chinese takeaway.'

'Why was your spare room turned into a Chinese takeaway?'

'You two, stop talking!' Dakin bawled. I faced front. 'So rich is the language in this Bible,' he said more quietly, 'that I haven't even chosen a section for us to look at because I know that I can open it at any point and find something uplifting, something poetic, something—'

'Boring?' said Ryan.

'Detention, Ryan,' said Dakin.

'Wicked,' said Ryan, grinning round like a hero.

'I shall demonstrate.' Face-Ache flipped open the Bible on his desk. 'Here we are, a completely random selection. Second Book of Kings. Turn to page four-two-five, everyone.'

Lots of rustling paper.

'Turn to it with *care*. These pages are delicate.'

Lots more rustling. *Lots* more. With any luck we could stretch it out to the end of the lesson.

'Have you all got it?' Dakin said wearily after ten minutes' rustling.

'What page, sir?' Atkins asked.

'Four hundred and twenty-five.'

'Twenty-five?' said Hislop.

'Yes,' said Dakin.

'Four **hundred** and twenty-five?' said Pete, who sits next to me.

'Yes!' Dakin screamed. 'Now if you've all managed to find the page, I want each of you to stand up and read a verse in turn.'

Another class-wide groan. 'Oh, not reading *aloud*!'

'Yes, reading aloud. Starting at the front here with you, Julia.'

'Me?' gasped orange-haired, orange-freckled Julia

Frame. 'Can't someone else go first?'

'Someone else can go **second**,' Face-Ache said firmly. 'Chapter nine, verse one. Arise and begin.'

Julia clunked to her feet. She was about to start reading when a phone rang.

Dakin's shoulders went up. His eyes shrank to pinheads.

'WHOSE IS THAT?!'

Six boys stood up at once, not to admit the phone was theirs, but to point at Pete, who was fumbling in his pocket trying to turn the thing off.

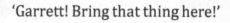

'Garrett! Bring that thing here!'

Pete got up. Took the mobile out of his pocket. Carried it to the front, where Dakin snatched it and chucked it in a drawer. 'Detention!' he said as Pete sauntered back to his seat. 'Now Julia, chapter nine, verse one. And read *clearly* please.'

Julia looked at the Bible, started to mumble.

'I said *clearly*,' Dakin said.

'This *is* clearly,' said Julia.

'Not to my ears, it isn't.'

'You can get them syringed at the Med Centre, sir,' I said. 'Doesn't hurt, just blows your brains out.'

'McCue should know,' said Pete. 'He's had it done twice.'

Start again,' Dakin said to Julia. 'And let us *hear* you this time.'

Julia started again. We couldn't hear a word, but no one complained, not even Face-Ache until she started the next verse.

'Just verse one, Julia. Angela?'

Angie stood up. She sits next to Julia. Pete and I grinned at one another. No chance of missing verse two with old Ange reading. Her mouth's got a built-in megaphone.

'"And when thou comest thither,"' she bawled, '"look out there Jehu the son of Je-hosh-a-PHAT, the son of Nim...Nimi...Nimshi, and go in, and make him arise up from—"'

'**What** sort of language did he say this was?' someone muttered.

Soon, though, it had become a pretty smooth operation. When someone finished reading their verse and sat down, the next person crashed to his or her feet and read theirs, while the rest of us tried to keep the snores down.

Neil Downey got up to read his verse. '"And he arose, and went into the house; and he poured the oil on his head..."'

I looked at the next verse but one, which would be mine. Then I did a double-take, and gulped. Why me? I thought. Why **me**?

Downey sat down. Pete got up to do his bit.

'"And thou shalt smite the house of Ahab thy master, that I may avenge the blood of my servants the Muppets..."'

'I think you'll find that is "prophets", Mr Garrett.'

'Oh yeah. "And the blood of all the servants of the LORD, at the hand of, er...Jezebel?"'

He sat down. Silence fell. I hunched low in my chair, hoping Dakin wouldn't notice me.

'Up, McCue, up, keep it flowing, keep it flowing.'

A giggle from across the room. Someone had noticed my verse. Then a low ripple started as more and more people checked it out. Then Pete saw it.

'Oh boy. Ooooooh boy. This is gonna be *priceless*.'

'Can someone else do mine, sir?' I said. 'Bit of a sore throat today.'

'No excuses. On your feet, boy! Read!'

I got up. Cleared my throat.

'"For the whole house of Ahab shall perish,"' I read,
'"and I will cut off from Ahab him that pisseth against
the wall, and him that is shut up—"'

Pete slid under his desk. The rest of the class
exploded.

And guess who got detention for causing it?

chapter three

When the bell went Ryan, Pete and I stayed behind. There's a rule at our school that a kid can't do a detention the day he gets it. Has to take a note home to tell his parents he's been Bad and give them a chance to nag him to death. Dakin wrote our notes with a few angry stabs of his pen and threw them at us. 'Monday!' He gave Pete his mobile back with a warning that next time he'd be taken to the bike sheds and shot.

DETENTION!!
Misbehaviour
in class!!

Angie was waiting for us at the gates. Milo Dakin was with her, looking really cheesed off.

'Why the face like a horse, Milo?' I said. 'Wasn't you got detention.'

'I have detention every day of the week,' he said. 'You should try living with my dad.'

'I'd rather tattoo my chest with a power drill.'

Seeing as he was so down we went home his way instead of ours. He moaned about his dad every step of the way and we made sympathetic noises to try and cheer him up.

'*Fat Chance*, ladies and gentlemen! *Fat Chance*! Help the homeless!'

An ultra-thin kid of about eighteen with a shaggy black dog shoved a magazine for the homeless in our faces. We reared

28

back. Some days you can't move in our town without tripping over *Fat Chance* sellers and their dogs. They always have dogs.

'Got one,' I lied to the *Fat Chance* seller and his dog. 'At home.'

'Oh sure, and where've I heard *that* before?' muttered the *Fat Chance* seller.

'Woof-off,' said the dog.

'He's driving me bonkers,' said Milo as we walked on.

'Yeah, those *Fat Chance* sellers,' Pete said.

'He means his dad,' Angie said.

'I knew that. Just hoping he'd change the CD.'

Milo didn't change the CD. 'I don't know how much longer I can live my life in alphabetical order,' he said.

'Alphabetical order?' I said. 'How does that work, then?'

'It's his latest "Keep Dakin World Tidy" scheme. Everything in my wardrobe and chest of drawers is already colour co-ordinated, but last night he word-processed all these labels saying "Handkerchiefs, Pyjamas, Shirts, Socks, Underwear". Does that sound *sane* to you?'

Angie patted him on the shoulder. 'Parents and teachers, Milo. Make it up as they go along. Don't let him get you down.'

These wise words didn't seem to help. Milo mooched on, dragging his school bag. This wasn't like him. He usually took his old man in his stride with a merry grin and a wince. It was hard to know what to say to him in this mood, so we just dragged our bags and mooched with him. It was Angie who broke the moochy silence.

'Just look at the state of that place. It's like an Oxfam reject shop.'

I glanced at the big new luxury apartment building across the road. It had got a lot of people talking, that place, because no one knew who owned it. Some rich businessman, they said, who stood to make a killing but didn't want people to know. The flats weren't for sale, just rent, but a month's rent there would have probably bought our house and garden gnome.

'The luxury apartment block for filthy rich people looks like an Oxfam reject shop?' I said in surprise.

'I mean Mr Mann's bus shelter,' said Angie.

Mr Mann's bus shelter was on our side of the road, bang opposite the luxury apartment block. Mr Mann was the town tramp. He'd turned up out of nowhere five or six years earlier, spent the night in the bus shelter, and never moved out.
Summer,

winter, heatwave,

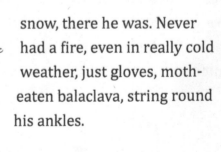

snow, there he was. Never had a fire, even in really cold weather, just gloves, moth-eaten balaclava, string round his ankles.

'What I wouldn't give to take a broom and duster to it,' Angie said.

'A match would be quicker,' said Pete.

It was a mess, though. Piles of old blankets and junk and litter, an ancient bookcase. Mr Mann was a great one for books. People gave him books all the time, and clothes and towels and stuff, though I don't think he ever asked. He had this thick tangled beard down to his waist, and thick tangled hair all down his back, tucked in the belt of his ratty old overcoat, which he wore in all weathers. But he was quite popular in spite of the way he looked and the state of his home. When the council tried to evict him last year there was a public outcry, so they dropped the idea and built a new shelter fifty metres along for people who actually want to catch buses.

'Hi, Mr Mann,' said Milo.

The raggedy old tramp looked up from his book and smiled.

'Hi, Milo. Good day at the workhouse?'

'Nah. You?'

'Oh, mustn't complain.'

Pete and Angie and I kept our eyes on the pavement. This wasn't our patch so we didn't know Mr Mann to speak to.

'You're very friendly with him,' Angie said when the bus shelter was behind us.

'He's a nice man,' Milo said. 'I often stop for a natter.' He sighed. 'I envy him. No responsibilities, no one telling him what to do the whole time.' He sighed again. 'P'raps I should give the Toilet of Life a go. Never know, might pick up a few tips on how to handle it. Life, I mean.'

'What's the Toilet of Life?' Angie asked.

'Computer game. I…I know the person who created it.'

Pete whirled round. 'You know someone who creates **computer games**?' Pete's a games nut.

'He only does it in his spare time,' Milo said. 'Just to keep his hand in. Used to be a scientist, something to do with genetics, but then he started his own games company, and...'

He stopped. Seemed kind of embarrassed, like he was betraying some kind of trust.

'This Toilet of Life,' said Pete. 'What's it all about?'

'I never played it,' Milo said. 'All I know is it's something to do with swapping your life for a better one.'

'Which is why you're so tempted,' I said.

He grunted.

'It's only a game, Milo,' Angie said. 'Won't change anything in the real world.'

'No, nothing changes that. You have no idea what it's like in our house. Everything has to be so *right* all the time.'

'Just when I thought we'd got on to something worth talking about,' Pete muttered.

'I mean *exactly* right,' Milo went on. 'Like, he doesn't believe in duvets so we have sheets and blankets, and I have to make my bed with the corners tucked under in perfect triangles, and my pyjamas have to be folded and smooth like they just came out of cellophane, and he goes ballistic if I put my elbows on the table at mealtimes, and did you ever hear of anyone else who has to eat spaghetti with a knife and fork?'

'Doesn't sound a whole lot of fun,' I said as we turned into Pizzle End Road and approached the Dakin residence.

'It isn't. Used to drive Mum even crazier than me. I'm not surprised she walked out. Just wish she'd taken me with her, is all.'

'Poor old Milo,' Angie said.

'And proper names,' he said, reaching his gate. 'The real names of things. No abbreviations, no nicknames or initials. Like, for instance, a television can't be called a TV in our house, oh no.'

'So what do you call it,' said Pete, 'a fridge?'

'He was the same with Mum,' Milo went on. 'She had to use the right words too, and everything had to be done the way he said, and the house had to be spotless the whole time, perfect, in case anyone visited.'

'And did they?' I asked.

'No.' He paused, then said, 'He wouldn't even let her have a dishwasher.'

'The brute,' said Ange.

'We haven't got a dishwasher either,' said Pete.

'You two have a lot in common then,' I said, grabbing Angie's arm and hauling her away to leave him and Milo to talk in peace about not having a dishwasher.

chapter four

Saturday morning. Fell out of bed and headed for the bathroom to see what the distorting mirror over the basin had to offer. Nothing good. The growth on my snoz had doubled in size overnight. Soon I'd need a periscope to see over it.

As I left the bathroom I met Dad yawning along the landing. I hadn't told him or Mum about Face-Ache's detention yet because I'd been waiting to get him on his own. When Mum hears I've been in trouble at school she comes over all disappointed and hurt like I'm letting her down personally or something, but Dad can usually handle it. Mum says this is because he's still a big kid himself.

'Hey, Dad,' I said. 'You know you're always saying how you used to get detentions at school all the time?'

'Ah yes.' His eyes misted over. 'Happiest days of my life.'

'Well I got one yesterday. In RE.'

'Detention in RE? How'd you manage that? Even I never had one of *those*.' He sounded impressed. 'What about love thy neighbour?'

'Doesn't apply to teachers and kids. I've got a note from Mr Dakin to tell you I'm in detention after school on Monday. You have to sign it.'

'Forge my signature,' Dad said. 'You know how it goes. Should do, you've used it often enough. So what did you do?'

I told him. The exact words.

He smirked. 'Things have changed since biblical days. Pretty common back then, pissething against walls. Nowadays we pisseth in lavatory pans, and flusheth afterwards.'

And he went into the bathroom to do just that. I went back to bed.

An hour later Mum threw my door back. She wasn't happy.

'Jiggy, your father tells me you've been given a detention in RE!'

I covered my head with the pillow. Mum tugged the pillow away and leaned over me with a hefty scowl.

'Well? What do you have to say for yourself?'

'I say it wasn't my fault. I only did what I was told.'

'Oh. Really. And I suppose you got detention for no reason.'

'Yes,' I said. 'Absolutely. Glad you understand.'

'All I understand,' she said, 'is that you're grounded for the day.'

'The day? Today? But Mum, it's Saturday!'

'Yes it is, and you will spend it catching up on all the homework you've so conveniently forgotten.'

'But that'll take Years!'

'Better get started then. And if you don't finish it to my satisfaction today you'll work on it tomorrow too.'

I managed to drag out most of the morning by eating breakfast

and getting dressed in slow motion,

but by early afternoon Mum had cottoned on to my cunning scheme and marched me up to my room and thrown my school books at me. So there I was, Saturday afternoon, day of rest number one, slaving away in my room and wondering how close I was to dying of boredom. I had my music up really loud to drown out the racket from downstairs. Dad was watching football down there, and when my dad's watching football the last place you want to be is the same house, or even the same street. I looked at the clock on the wall. Five past three. 'Hmm,' I said, 'mid-afternoon. Time to raid the biscuit tin and knock back a litre or two of fizz.'

I headed downstairs.

The noise got more and more unbelievable with every downward step. It was hard to tell who was making the most, the telly or Dad. I looked in the living room. There he was, the poor old Golden Oldie, shouting and punching the ceiling. Braindead United had scored. I was surprised to see that he wasn't alone today. Stallone was there too. Stallone usually makes himself scarce when football's on, like me when I have a choice – like my mother, who'd gone to the Garden Centre where she practically lives. But today Stallone was in and he didn't look too pleased about the peace-and-quiet famine. He was standing with his ears up, eyes like killer zap guns aimed at the middle-aged yob on the couch.

Dad wasn't aware of the effect he was having on the family pet. Too busy jumping up and down and screaming himself hoarse, arms in the air.

But then Stallone cracked. With an ear-splatting squeal of rage the furious cat flew across the room, landed on the innocent football fan's chest, and drove his claws deep into the armpits on either side. Dad's new scream wasn't much different from the old one except there was a tad less joy in it. He was still at it when Stallone raced back across the room and jumped out the window.

'That's it!' Dad shrieked. 'That cat is going to the vet's!'

I stared in horror. 'Dad. You wouldn't.'

He looked from one armpit to the other. Blood was seeping through his shirt. 'Watch me,' he growled.

'You can't,' I said. 'I mean yes, OK, he went a little over the top just then, but that's no reason to have him put down. Couldn't you just, say...cut his meat ration for a while?'

Dad looked up from his armpits. His eyes were almost as red as they were. He gave a dry little chuckle.

'I won't have him put down. That'd be too good for him. No, I'll have him done.'

'Done?'

'Neutered. Doctored. Separated from his cherries. If that doesn't calm him down, nothing will. It'd certainly take the edge off my day.'

But then a dim little spot of sanity returned to his eyes.

'Don't tell your mother though, will you? She wouldn't approve.'

'You told her about my detention.'

He looked suddenly shifty. 'I had to. Can't keep school stuff from your mum, you know that. And I didn't tell her what you did to her plant, did I?'

'That wasn't my fault. Stallone tripped me.'

'Stallone again,' Dad said. 'You have to admit, that cat's a liability. If we have him seen to he'll be calmer. Less mean. Come on, Jig, say you won't tell your mum Stallone's heading for the nutcracker.'

'She's bound to find out sooner or later,' I said.

The mad look flashed back into his eyes. A thin tight smile jerked his lips to left and right.

'By then it'll be too late. The little monster'll be as docile as a fluffy pyjama case.'

With that he fell back on the couch looking from one bloody pit to the other, and began whimpering quietly.

chapter five

When Mum returned from the Garden Centre and found Dad whingeing on the couch with his arms in the air, she drove him to the hospital for a tetanus jab. When she brought him back his arms were down but they still wouldn't hang properly because the bandages in his armpits were the size of bricks.

'Has the vicious little fiend come back yet?' he asked me.

'If you mean Stallone, I haven't seen him. He's probably keeping out of your way.'

'Very wise.'

After tea I was about to slip over to Angie's and Pete's when my mother threw herself across the front door.

'No you don't, my lad. Grounded I said and grounded I meant.'

'Until I caught up with my homework, you said.'

Her face went all narrow and suspicious. 'Are you saying you have?'

'Absolutely, now step aside please.'

'You're not leaving this house until I've checked it over.'

'The house?'

'The homework. If it's not up to scratch you can do it again.'

She walked me back to my room and went through my homework. Slowly. Made me do a couple of bits again too, so it was getting late by the time I was finally allowed out. Over the road I rang Pete and Angie's bell.

Pete opened the door. 'Hi, scumbag.'

'Whose room?' I said, barging past him.

'Mine.'

We started up the stairs. 'Where's Angie?'

'Bath, hairwash. Usual Saturday night girlie stuff. Coming along a treat, that.'

'What is?'

'The giant fairy light on your nose.'

Up in his room he flopped into the swivel chair in front of his PC.

'What are you doing?'

'Writing my diary,' he answered, typing.

'You keep a diary? What do you put in it?'

'All the really terrific and exciting stuff that happens round here.'

He leaned back so I could read what he'd just written.

Saturday. Did nothing. Evening. Jiggy here. Typed this.

'And these are the best years of our lives,' I said sadly.

'Hey – life!' Pete said.

'What about it?'

'That game Milo mentioned. The Toilet of Life. Let's check it out.'

I'm not into computer games myself, but there wasn't much else to do, so I said, 'OK,' and waited while Pete typed

in the search window. And there it was. Then he clicked something and a door appeared. A notice on the door said '**Vacant**'.

'What now?' I said. Pete clicked the notice. The door swung inward and we were looking at a large toilet with the seat down. Scrawled on the wall behind the toilet, like graffiti, were the words:

The Toilet of Life
A Manx Game

There were no instructions, no clues what to do next, so Pete clicked around a bit more. Nothing happened until he clicked on the toilet's handle. It moved, the toilet flushed, and suddenly the screen was chock-a-block with much smaller toilets, all with their seats down, and weaving in and out of them were all these little people.

'Wonder what happens next?' Pete said.

He started clicking all over again. At first the result was the same as before – nothing – but then one of the tiny toilet seats flew up and the nearest little person gave a yelp and jumped head first into the bowl. He was halfway in, legs kicking wildly, looked stuck there, but then there was this miniature flushing sound and he slithered all the way down.

'How did you do that?' I asked.

'Dunno, but if I can do it once...'

He clicked away, searching for the hidden trigger that made the little people jump into the toilets and get flushed. A second seat flew up. A second little person yelped, jumped in, kicked, and was flushed away.

'Think I've got it,' Pete said, and clicked some more.

'Hey Jig.'

I turned with relief as Angie came in. Her hair was up in a towel and she was wearing shiny black pyjamas covered in stars and planets and comets and stuff.

'Hey Ange.'

'What's he up to?'

'That game Milo Dakin was thinking of trying. The Toilet of Life.'

'Any good?'

'Nah. Just another zapfest. Death and destruction but with toilets.'

We looked for somewhere to sit. This is always a problem in Pete's room because he likes to decorate the carpet with clothes, comics and all sorts of junk. The only other place was the bed but you wouldn't catch us on that – Pete's disgusting feet had been in it – so we cleared a space on the floor and parked our back ends. While Pete flushed and whooped like a maniac in the corner I told Angie about Mad-Cat Stallone and my father's armpits.

'He says he's going to
have him vetted,' I said.
'Stallone's privates
are going to be
toast.'

'Bit drastic.'

'Just a bit.'

'Hey, come and
look at this,' Pete said.

'We're not interested
in people being flushed
down toilets,' I said.

'The people are all flushed. Now another toilet's
turned up, with a message.'

'What sort of message?'

'Come and see.'

We went across and looked at the screen. The people and the little toilets had disappeared. Their place had been taken by a much bigger toilet, a twin of the one we'd found behind the 'Vacant' door. Wafting round it was a banner with these words:

FEEL THAT YOUR LIFE HAS GONE DOWN THE PAN?

WELL HERE'S YOUR CHANCE TO SWAP IT FOR A BETTER ONE.

JUST INVITE SOMEONE ROUND WHO'S REALLY GOT IT MADE AND HIT

'F for FLUSH'!

'So this is what Milo meant,' I said.

'Yeah,' said Pete, stretching a finger towards **'F for Flush'**.

'Leave it alone,' Angie said. 'We don't know what it is.'

But she was curious too, and maybe she would have let him hit **'F for Flush'** if not for a sudden shout from Pete's dad.

'Pete! Why haven't you washed up yet?'

Pete went to the door. 'Five minutes!'

'No minutes! It's your turn and it should have been done. Kitchen, rubber gloves, five seconds, or you're in the deep stuff!'

'Nobody hit "**F for Flush**" while I'm gone, right?' Pete said.

'Wouldn't want to,' said Ange.

Pete went. I peered at the screen. The toilet seat was quivering, like it was itching to open. My '**F for Flush**' finger twitched.

'Don't, Jig,' Angie said. 'I have a funny feeling about this.'

'It's just a gimmick,' I said. 'Come on, let's give it a go.'

'It says "**Feel that your life has gone down the pan**". Your life isn't so bad.'

'Not so bad? With a homework tyrant for a mother,

an armpit-eating cat,

and a meteorite on my nose?

Swap with you any day.'

'At least you have a *father*,' Angie said.

'He's all yours,' I said, and hit '**F for Flush**'.

The toilet seat flew up and a bright blue cloud shot out. The cloud fanned across the screen until it filled it, corner to corner, and then...

...it started spewing into the room.

'Impossible,' I said.

'Told you something would happen,' said Angie.

'But it's a computer game. No computer game is so interactive it can come into the room.'

More and more of the blue stuff seeped out.

'Didn't Milo say the designer used to be some sort of scientist?' Angie said.

'So?'

'So maybe he added something extra. Something to make it *really* interactive. I say we get out of here.'

We glanced towards the door. The blue cloud swirled between us and it.

'Only other way out's the window,' I said.

We turned to the window. The blue cloud was there too.

We were trapped.

'Jig, when we do get out of here,' Angie said, 'I want you to remind me to do something.'

'What's that?'

'Remove your teeth with pliers one by one.'

We were still standing there wondering what to do next when the two halves of the cloud joined up and covered us. It was like being in a blue fog. Seconds later, all these sparkly bits started appearing. Then they were bursting – pop-pop-pop – like thousands of tiny balloons. And when they burst…

'What a *stink*!' Angie said.

She was right. No nostril could survive that for long.

Pop-pop-pop.

'I'm out of here,' I said, groping for the door.

Instead of the door I found Angie, also groping. We slapped one another's hands for a while, then yanked the door back and stepped outside. As we closed the door to keep the stink and the cloud in, the Toilet of Life flushed – loudly. We stumbled downstairs, ripped the front door open, and gulped air.

'Feel sorta queasy,' Angie said quietly.

'Me too,' I said. 'And...sleepy.'

'Gotta hit the sack,' said Ange.

'Likewise.'

While she went back upstairs, clawing the banister, I stumbled out into the street wishing I had a banister of my own. In two minutes I was home, up in my room. In three I was hopping about trying to slot a foot into a pyjama leg. In four and three-quarter minutes I was in bed. In five I was sleeping peacefully. Well, not so peacefully. I had a dream. A dream that I was being pulled down into this enormous toilet by grasping hands.

And flushed away.

chapter six

and now we come to the morning it **really** started. I woke up feeling kind of strange. Not myself somehow. But at least it wasn't a school day. My head was deep inside the duvet when I heard my mother's voice yelling from downstairs.

'Jiggy! Your father's gone to watch two-a-side football and I'm off to the Garden Centre to look at water features! Don't lie there all day!'

I waited for the front door to slam before heading for the bathroom to make a water feature of my own. I still felt sort of peculiar, like part of me was... well, missing. One thing that was definitely missing was the growth on my nose. Good news, I thought, stroking my smooth lump-free beak.

I was almost at the bathroom when I caught a sly movement on the stairs. Stallone – creeping up them. First I'd seen of him since yesterday. A shiver of fear tap-danced through me. The great armpit massacre might have given him a taste for human

 blood and he wanted some of mine now. But he didn't attack me. Far from it. When he got to the top of the stairs he wound himself round my ankles so tight that I couldn't go another step. And he purred. If you knew

Stallone you'd know how rare this is. Purring just never happens when he's near me or Dad. But I saw what he was after. He wanted to get me on his side.

'Won't work,' I told him. 'No sympathy for you. You only have yourself to blame.'

I eased my ankles out of his furry grip and continued along the landing for twelve full centimetres before I heard what I'd just said and came to a shocked halt. Well, not **what** I'd said, but **how**. What was wrong with my *voice*?

Just then the phone on the wall rang. I considered ignoring it, but it kept on and on so I grabbed it to shut it up.

'What!'

'Jiggy?'

'Who's that?' I said with my new peculiar voice.

'Angie.'

'You don't sound like Angie.'

'You don't sound like Jiggy. We have to meet. Come to the door.'

'Soon as I'm dressed,' I said.

'Come as you are!' she yelled. '*NOW!!!*'

The phone died. I sighed, but obediently jogged down – and on the way felt something else peculiar. I've jogged down those stairs a million times but it felt all wrong today, like my lower decks had gone to the Bahamas without me.

I opened the door wishing I wasn't still in my pyjamas. Across the road Pete and Angie's door was already open and someone stood there looking at me. Someone in snazzy black PJs with stars and planets all over them. Not Angie though. Someone else.

Me.

I clutched the door handle to stop my knees giving way. As I clutched, I half turned and caught a glimpse of myself in the hall mirror.

The face in the mirror wasn't mine.

It was Angie's.

I looked back across the road. At myself in Angie's fancy pyjamas. I was puzzled. Too puzzled to be horrified. Horror would start about twenty-five seconds later when it sank in. Well I ask you. Would *your* mind be working on full power if you'd just woken up and discovered that you'd switched bodies with the kid across the road?

A kid of the opposite *sex*?

chapter seven

angie was properly dressed when she came over. Well, properly. Her clothes on my body. Looked kind of wrong somehow. Naturally Pete found it all a real hoot. It was all right for him, he still had his own body, but it was no picnic for me having to walk round with Angie Mint's girlie apparatus. You don't need Sex Education lessons to know there are serious differences between boys and girls. Actually, knowing all the gory details made it even worse somehow. I'd seen the diagrams. I'd looked at the pictures of the internal workings with a magnifying glass. But now that I was so close to everything, using it like it was my own, I felt kind of...unwell.

I soon found out that Angie didn't feel much happier, even though she had the better end of the deal.

'This is your fault,' she said, with my voice.

'How do you make that out?' I said, with hers.

'Well it wasn't *me* who hit "F for Flush".'

'You think the Toilet of Life did this?'

'Can you think of anything else that's invited you to swap lives with the person standing next to you recently?'

'Lives,' I said. 'Didn't say anything about bodies.'

'Same difference. I told you not to fiddle with it, but would you listen? Oh no.'

'I wonder...' said Pete.

'Wonder what?' I asked.

'If the Toilet of Life could be some new kind of computer virus.'

'Computer viruses ruin your hard disk, not your life. Corrupt your files, not your genes.'

'Yeah, but technology's advancing all the time. Never know what they'll come up with next. If it is a virus that can travel round the Internet and infect people through their home computers...wow, talk about progress!'

'*Progress?*' Angie and I said, gazing helplessly at our bodies on the wrong people.

'Well, progress or not,' she said, 'until we figure out what to do about it we have to pretend to be each other. Come on,' she said to me. 'Upstairs. We have to swap clothes.'

'You want to swap **_clothes_** with me now?' I said in dismay.

'Looking the way we do, we have to,' she said.

We went up. Pete too, chuckling quietly.

'I think we need a few ground rules in case we can't

reverse this for a while,' Angie said as we reached the landing.

'What sort of ground rules?'

'No peeking, for one. That's my private property you have there, copyright Angie Mint. If you have to get changed in daylight or with the light on keep your eyes on the ceiling. No taking baths or showers either. At last you have a genuine excuse. You only do stuff you really have to, and you don't hang about doing that. Got it?'

'Got it,' I said, 'and ditto.' We went into my room. 'In fact double ditto. You have one extra little attachment I wish I didn't have to mention.'

'Clothes!' Angie snarled.

I grabbed my things from the chair I'd thrown them at last night.

Angie curled my lip. 'Not *used* ones.'

'I was never that picky when I was a boy,' I said, but opened some drawers and hauled out a clean shirt, jeans, socks, Y-fronts.

'You can keep the undies,' she said.

'It's all right,' I said, 'they're new. My mother bought six pairs of fire-damaged pants from this vandalised warehouse sale. Besides, you have to wear some. They're specially designed to cope with the free extra attachment.'

'The escape hatch comes in handy,' Pete pointed out.

Angie snatched the clothes, including the fire-damaged Ys, and flung herself out of the room.

'Where ya going?' I shouted after her.

'Bathroom!' she shouted back. 'To change!'

'I've seen it all before, you know. Quite often actually.'

'Not on me, you haven't.' She was about to go in when she thought of something. 'Jig, you haven't... you know, been to the...?'

'Had to,' I said. 'Don't worry, I sat through the whole thing.'

She slammed the bathroom door. Half a minute later it opened a fraction and slung her clothes out.

'Clean on fifteen minutes ago,' she said, and slammed the door again.

Clean or not, she could keep the girlie undies. There was a limit. I carried them to my room between finger and thumb and kicked them into the Twilight

Zone under my bed. Pete watched, grinning like the village idiot.

I pointed at the door. 'Out!'

He went, chortling.

I got dressed as quickly as I could with my eyes shut. I'd had about twenty minutes to get used to this but I still couldn't believe it was happening. I mean, imagine. There you are a boy all your life, you hit the hay one night and next morning there's a lot of slack in the fire-damaged Y-fronts. Something like that takes a bit of mental adjustment.

When Angie came out of the bathroom in my clothes she marched straight up to me and swiped me round the head. It might have been her head, but it was me who felt it.

'What was that for?'

She pointed angrily at her new nose.

'Oh,' I said. 'That.'

The thrill of finding I'd turned into a girl in my sleep had put the huge spot quite a way down my list of things to get worked up about. It was so big today, so red and squishy, that you couldn't really call it a spot any more.

'Looks like a boil now,' I said.

'Very big boil,' said Pete.

'Big as a house,' I said.

'Detached,' said Pete.

'And guess what, Ange,' I said.

'What?' she said.

'It's all yours.'

chapter eight

We considered telling our parents what had happened. But not for long. You can't tell your Golden Oldies you've swapped bodies with a neighbour and expect them to carry on as normal. Their poor old brains can't handle stuff like that. No, this was something we had to deal with ourselves.

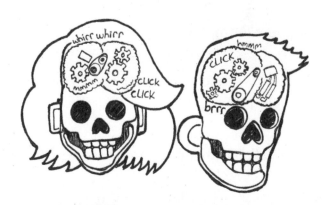

'We need to think this through,' I said. 'But not here. I don't know what I'd do if Mum or Dad waltzed in and saw me like this.'

'They'd think you were me,' Angie said.

'Exactly. We need to be on neutral ground while we get used to this.'

'How about the park?'

'Fine.'

'Have to be careful on the way though,' she said. 'Pretend we're who we look like in case we bump into anyone we know.'

'No problem for me,' said Pete.

'You mean if we meet someone I have to talk the way you would?' I said.

'Not just talk,' said Angie. 'You have to *be* me. If

you look like me but act like you people will think something's up.'

'Something is up, Ange. Very up.'

'Yes, well let's stop whining and make the best of it, shall we?'

'Best?' I said. 'What best? There is no best.'

She came over all fierce.

'Pull yourself together, McCue. Where's your backbone?'

'Turn round, I'll show you.'

But I saw her point. If we didn't act like one another people might stare. Then they might ask questions. We could do without questions.

We left the house and set off, trying to be each other.

It wasn't easy. I mean I've known Angie since before I can remember, but I've never taken much notice of the way she moves and all. She seemed to be having a bit of trouble being me too.

'Angie,' I said, 'don't take this the wrong way, but put a lid on the strut, eh? You're killing my image here.'

She narrowed my eyes at me. 'How do you mean?'

'Well Jiggy McCue's a pretty cool dude, and—'

'News to me,' said Pete.

'—and cool-as-a-cube Jig just doesn't walk like that.'

'So how am I walking that's so uncool?'

'Kind of hunched over and swinging my arms like something in a wildlife documentary with fleas. This isn't a criticism of you personally, you understand.'

'What about you then? You've started to mince.'

'Mince?'

'Walk with dear little steps and waggle my hips.'

'Get outta here.'

'He's mincing, isn't he?' she said to Pete.

Pete nodded. 'Like a maniac.'

'Look, I'm doing my best here,' I said. 'You think it's easy being a female?'

'Half the population seem to manage it,' Angie said.

'Yeah, the other half. And will you stop pouting?'

'Pouting? I don't pout.'

'Didn't used to,' I said. 'Not that I noticed anyway. Maybe my lips don't agree with you.'

'Don't get your knickers in a twist,' Pete said to me with a punchable smirk.

By this time Ange and I were doing our bad impressions of each other close to Mr Mann's bus shelter.

'Wonder who he is?' Angie said.

'Mr Mann,' I said.

'I mean the bloke talking to him.'

The bloke talking to Mr Mann was an official-looking type in a suit who'd just taken a batch of papers out of his briefcase and handed them to Mr Mann.

'Could be someone from the council sent to have another stab at getting him to sling his hook,' said Pete.

'On a Sunday?'

'Overtime. Double pay.'

The council type took a pen out of his pocket and handed it to Mr Mann, who scribbled something on one of the papers.

'Probably just signed his own eviction notice,' Angie said.

'Hello, Angie. Never seen you over this way before.'

We turned. Julia Frame, who sits next to Angie in class. Julia really irritates Angie. Whenever she's in a mood Julia tries to cheer her up with hugs and little songs, and Angie wants to thump her. Suddenly I understood this. Here we are trying not to meet anyone we know and she pops up out of the blue with her orange hair and freckles and a bunch of flowers, smiling.

At me.

'Shove off, Jools,' I said. 'We're having a private conversation here.'

Julia's sugar-sweet smile puckered. Her bottom lip trembled.

'Why are you so mean to me?' she said miserably.

I glanced at the others. Pete was grinning his head off, but Angie's expression wasn't so easy to read, even though it was one of mine.

Was that admiration I saw in my eyes? Maybe she was impressed. Thought I was doing a good job of being her.

'Mean?' I said to Julia. 'You want mean, stick around. If you don't, let's see your dust.'

She blinked, tears in her eyes. 'But I lent you my Barbie pencil sharpener.'

'And...?' I said.

'Well I don't lend just *anyone* my pencil sharpener.'

'I'm touched. Now beat it or I call the cops.'

A little sob burst like a bubble from her mouth. She spun round and walked away with her head about waist-high. I felt good about that for three whole seconds. Then I came over guilty as hell. For some reason I couldn't look at Angie. I felt – don't laugh – ashamed.

'Hey Julia!' I yelled after her. 'Nice flowers! Who are they for?'

'They're for someone who *cares* about me!' she shouted back with a trembly voice. 'My nan, for her birthday! She's over fifty, she'll be dead soon, then I'll be really upset and you can make even more fun of me!'

It was all I could do not to break down myself as she walked away. Me, Jiggy McCue, all set to blub his eyes out. Well, Angie's eyes. Hey now, wait. What was going on here? Angie never got all emotional about stuff, not soppy emotional, but I was using her equipment, so why had Julia got to me when she wouldn't have got to Ange? I needed to think about this, but not now.

'That girl's a nutter,' I said, super-cool.

I glanced at Pete, expecting him to agree with me. His grin was gone. He was gaping at me in horror.

'Nice *flowers*? Since when did you notice *flowers*?'

'Well I...'

He was right, of course. I'm a boy. Flowers live in another universe. I looked at Angie. Her expression was easy enough to read now. It told me that she knew what I was going through. Knew but wasn't sympathetic. Suddenly I realised something. Angie had all the emotional stuff that girls are born with but she didn't give in to it. She kept it inside, deep inside, refused to let it out. Looking at her now, head held high, shoulders back, you'd never have guessed she was a girl this time yesterday. She made a much better boy than I ever did.

chapter nine

It wasn't until we were almost at the park that I realised I wasn't living up to my name. I mean I'm not called Jiggy for nothing. For the first two or three years of my life I couldn't keep still for a minute. My parents thought there was something wrong with me. They took me to experts. The experts were stumped at first. Then they came to this Big Conclusion. 'He has too much energy, but he's too lazy to put it to proper use.' What they meant was that instead of doing normal boy stuff like getting into fights and kicking balls around between every meal I danced on the spot and made rapper-type arm movements all over the place. I've got it more under control these days, but I still move around quite a bit when stuff happens. Turning into a girl without an operation should have sent me jigging all the way up to the roof, you'd think. But it didn't. Not one part of me had jigged since I inherited Angie's body.

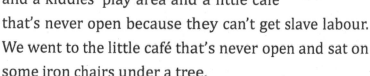

The Councillor Snit Memorial Park is quite big and open. It has tennis courts and a kiddies' play area and a little café that's never open because they can't get slave labour. We went to the little café that's never open and sat on some iron chairs under a tree.

'We have to talk,' I said.

'Must we?' said Ange.

'Yes. I think we need to give the Toilet of Doom another flush.'

'Toilet of Life,' she corrected.

'Life? You call this life? Doom I said and Doom I meant.'

'Whatever. You think another flush might reverse this?'

'It's worth a try and it's all we have. Do you remember how you flushed away all the little people?' I asked Pete.

'Sure, why?'

'Well, it wasn't till all the little people had gone down all the little pans that the big toilet with the "**F for Flush**" invitation came up. So obviously you have to flush the little people again to give us another go at "**F for Flush**". Right?'

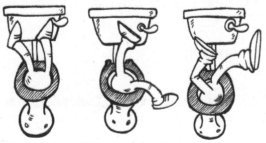

'What's in it for me?' he said.

'What do you mean, what's in it for you? You're our mate, Three Musketeers, one for all and all for lunch.'

'This is business. Toilet business. Come on, what are you offering?'

'Will this do?' Angie said, raising one of my fists.

Pete jumped out of his chair – 'Have to catch me first!' – and scooted up the tree we sat under.

'Like that's a problem?' Angie said, and scooted up after him.

He was out of his tiny mind if he thought he could escape Angie just by climbing a tree. She's always been better at tree-climbing than Pete – or me – and she was even better at it in my body for some reason. They both vanished into the leaves, which immediately started shaking like crazy. Then Pete started yelling and suddenly...

THUDD!

... he was lying at my feet. Angie dropped down from the tree and Pete rolled onto his side, pulled his knees into his chest, and crossed his arms over his head half a second before she started pummelling him.

I leaned back in my iron chair, smiling. The sun was out, there was a bit of a breeze, birds gargled, and one of my best friends was being beaten up by my other best friend. It was good to be alive. Suddenly I realised that everything seemed so much brighter than usual. More interesting somehow. I don't think I ever looked at a tree or bush before and thought,

Hey, cool tree, cool bush. And the smells. The grass, the air, those things with petals. Was this what it was like for real girls? If so, all I can say is no wonder most of them are quieter in class and not thumping one another all the time and cheeking the teachers.

After a while Angie got fed up of pummelling someone who didn't fight back and let Pete up. They slumped back in their seats. Pete was puffing a bit.

'Do you mind if I say something, Ange?' I said gently.

She glared at me. 'Depends what.'

'Well, don't take this the wrong way, but you're a bit violent today.'

'Violent?'

'Yes. I mean you always had a temper, but—'

'Temper?' she said, folding my hands into fists. 'Whaddayamean **temper**?!'

'Angela,' I said. 'A warthog with a bad home-life has a better temper than you, even on your good days.'

She aimed a swipe at me, but I ducked in time.

'See?' I said.

Surprisingly, she did. And came over sort of shocked. All the anger and aggression drained out of her.

'You're right,' she said. 'Ever since I got this miserable excuse for a body I've felt...tense. My hands – your hands – keep balling up into fists and wanting to bash things. You know what it is, don't you?'

'No, what?'

'Testosterone.'

'The chocolate bar?'

'Testosterone, you prat, not Toblerone.'

'Teswotterone?' said Pete.

'Testosserone,' I told him.

'You don't have any idea what it is, do you?' Angie said. I shrugged. She looked amazed: 'Don't you two pay attention in *any* lessons?'

'Try not to,' said Pete.

'I'm talking human biology,' she said. 'I'm talking hormones.'

'I know about hormones,' I said. 'Stallone has them.'

'Stallone?'

'Yeah. Dad says that if Stallone didn't have so many hormones he wouldn't be half as vicious and mean.'

'You want to get back to testosterone?' Angie said.

'Didn't know we'd left it,' I said.

Angie ground my teeth to powder and started again.

'Testosterone, in moron terms, is something males have a lot of and females don't. Something that makes them want to fight all the time and disrupt lessons. Makes them mad for fast cars and martial arts videos. Makes them *violent*.'

'I'm not like that,' I said.

'You can be a pain in class.'

'Naturally, I'm only human, but not the other stuff. Fast cars, martial arts, violence. I was never into any of that when I was a boy.'

'That's because you were a wimp,' she said.

'No, no. It was my hormones. Made me jig about instead, that's all.'

'You're not jigging now,' Pete said.

'The jig seems to go with the body, and that's out on loan. Only it doesn't make you jig,' I said to Angie. 'Makes you want to slug people.'

'Yes,' she said, pacing up and down. 'I can't help myself. God, I'd love a good fight right now!'

'Keep away from me,' Pete said.

'I said *good* fight.' She stopped pacing. Stared helplessly at us. 'I think I'm turning into a psychopath.'

'You could be right,' I said. 'Much longer on my testosserstuff and who knows what sort of monster you'll turn into.'

She shook herself. 'We have to re-flush the Toilet of Doom and get our bodies back! Right away!'

'That's what I was saying a while ago.'

'Yes! And now I'm saying it!'

'We don't know it'll work,' I pointed out calmly.

'No, but it's all there is. We've got to try!'

'If it doesn't we could be stuck like this,' I said, still calm. 'Then what?'

'Then one day Angie orders her first martial arts video,' Pete said, 'and you accompany her mum to the bra stall on the market.'

I stopped being calm. I leapt up. So did Angie. We raced neck-and-neck for the park gates. Got home a good twenty minutes before Pete ambled in wiping tears of joy from his eyes.

chapter ten

We stood behind Pete while he called up the Toilet of Life. The door with the notice on it appeared. But today the notice on the door didn't say '**Vacant**'. It said '**Engaged**'. Pete clicked it anyway.

The door didn't open.

He clicked again. Still didn't.

'Oh, you're useless,' said Angie.

She hoicked him out of the chair, took his place, and clicked '**Engaged**'.

The door stayed shut. She clicked again.

Still shut.

'We seem to have a teensy problem,' I said.

'You give up too easily!' she said.

She clicked 'Engaged' another thousand times, less and less feverishly as time went on, before sitting back, chewing my lip.

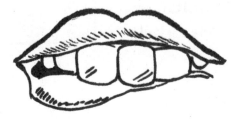

'It doesn't want to open,' she said at last.

'Milo knows the geezer who created it,' Pete said.

'Maybe he could introduce us. The creator's bound to know how to get the door open.'

It was the best idea any of us had had. It was also the only idea.

If Milo's dad had been someone else we might have had their landline number, but he wasn't so we hadn't. They were in the book, though.

'Pete, give me your mobile,' Angie said.

'Where's yours?'

'Somewhere else.'

He handed over his phone. 'What if Face-Ache answers?' I said.

'I ask for Milo, what do you think?'

But Face-Ache didn't answer.

'Hello? Milo?' Angie said, with my voice. 'It's Angie.'

'Jiggy,' I said, with hers.

'Yeah, Jiggy,' she said. 'Listen, Milo. You know that game you mentioned the other day, the Toilet of Doom?'

'Life,' said Pete.

'Toilet of Life,' said Ange.

We put our ears close to the receiver so we could hear his reply.

'Funny you should mention that,' Milo said.
'I was talking only yesterday to…my friend who created it. He brought it up actually, and…' He stopped. 'Woh. Hey. You haven't been fooling with it, have you?'

'We took a look out of curiosity,' Angie said. 'Couldn't get the toilet door open.'

'Oh, that'll be the glitch.'

'Glitch?'

'My friend says it's not working the way it should. It jams, then suddenly starts up again and goes rogue.'

'Rogue? What does that mean?'

'Doesn't do what it's meant to. It started out as an ordinary game, he says, but it's proving too clever for its own good. My friend said I'd better not mess with it till he's sorted it out. You'd better not either.'

'Us?' Angie said, scowling at me. 'No chance. Got more sense.'

'Look, Jig,' Milo said to her. 'I can't talk now. My dad's really rattling me. Know what he's doing now? Ironing his shoelaces. I don't think I can take much more of this.'

He hung up.

Angie and I sank to the floor to await the end of the world. Pete didn't join us. His world was still going strong. He threw himself on the bed, put his hands under the back of his head, and grinned at the ceiling.

'I can't wait for tomorrow,' he said.

'Why, what happens tomorrow?' I asked.

'School. Be such a laugh. For me anyway. Not so much for you two. Specially Jiggy.'

'Why specially me?'

'You'll be the one in the skirt.'

'Skirt?' I said. 'Whoa. No. Not me.'

'Girls have to wear skirts to school, it's the rules,' Angie said.

'Yeah, but I'm not a girl. Not really.'

'You look like one.'

'But I'm not, that's the point.'

'No, that *is* the point. You look like a girl so you have to dress like one. It's the *way* it works.'

'But even the skirt's not the best bit,' Pete said cheerfully.

'There's *more*?' I wailed.

'Oh *yes*!' he sang. 'What do we do Monday afternoons?'

'Monday aftern...?'

I realised. On Monday afternoons the boys play football with Mr Rice and the girls do other things with Miss Weeks. I glanced at Angie, expecting her to be as horrified as me. But she seemed to have perked up a bit.

'Football with Rice,' she mused. 'Could be interesting.'

'Oh yes,' I said. 'Right. Just what you've always wanted, isn't it? Free license to kick boys where it hurts, shove their faces in the mud and all. But what about me? Do you realise what I'll have to **wear**?'

'Yep,' said Pete, picturing it.

I'd probably have been pretty amused too if he'd been in my position. But he wasn't. It was me who was going to have to wear little green knickers and a shortie gym skirt.

'I'm taking tomorrow off,' I said.

'You can't,' said Ange. 'If you don't go they'll think it's me not going.'

'Think what they like, I'm not going – tomorrow or any other day that I have to be you.'

She clenched my fists and narrowed my eyes at me.

'You're going,' she said, 'if I have to drag you by the hair and stuff you into my Games kit personally.'

'You sound like my mother,' I said. 'You *look* more like my father. But you sound like my mother.'

'Ooh, I won't be able to sleep tonight,' said Pete.

'*You* won't be able to sleep?' I said.

'No. The way it's looking, tomorrow's going to be the highlight of my entire school career.'

There was only one thing that made life worth living just then: the thought that I wouldn't have to do my detention tomorrow. Angie would have to do it for me. I didn't mention this. Not yet. It wasn't much, but I needed something to look forward to.

chapter eleven

now that Angie and I were supposed to be one another we had to swap houses. And rooms. The only good thing about this for me was that Angie hates girlie stuff. I would have screamed myself to sleep if I'd had to jog to Dreamland in a frilly nightie. Still, as I was turning in that night I fell to my knees and prayed to the great toilet in the sky to flush my body back to me while I slept. You might not be surprised to hear that when I woke up next morning and found for the umpteenth time that prayers don't work, I did not fling back the duvet with a hearty cheer and hang party balloons.

To avoid being caught doing something un-Angie by the resident Golden Oldies, I kept out of their way as much as possible and hung about upstairs until they left for work. When I went down I wore Angie's dressing gown over her school uniform. Pete was in the kitchen stuffing himself with Chocolate Cheerios in chocolate milk with a chocolate flake crumbled on top. Pete likes chocolate.

'Lemme see,' he said, tugging at the front of Angie's dressing gown.

I slapped his hand. 'Get off.'

By the time we left for school I'd got more used to my new outfit (which in a way was more comfortable than my usual, but don't tell anyone).

'Don't forget this,' Pete said.

Angie's sports bag dangled from his fingers. I snatched it off him.

'Hey, what do I call you?' he said as we crossed the road.

'Call me?'

'Well I can't call you Jiggy. Not in public. Have to be Angie.'

'Call me Angie just once and you're a chalk outline on the tarmac.'

We reached the opposite pavement. I looked at my ex-house. I paused.

'I'll wait here,' I said.

'Be bold!' said Pete, and lugged me up the path. He pressed the bell. 'Hair looks nice,' he said as we stood side by side on the step.

The door was opened by my mother. Dad stood behind her looking sorry for himself, hands on hips to give his armpits room to breathe.

'Hello Pete, hello Angie,' said Mum.

Pete grunted, like he does.

Not me though. I speak when spoken to.

'Hello Mum, hello Dad.'

My mother's eyebrows somersaulted over the back of her head.

'Twit,' Pete said out of the side of his mouth.

I laughed – 'Ha-ha-ha' – and said, "I mean hello Peg, hello Mel.'

Mum clawed her eyebrows back and smiled.

'Mum-Dad, Peg-Mel, what does it matter? We've all known one another so long we're like one big happy family now.'

'Happy?' my father cried, flinging his hands at the ceiling. 'Have you seen my **armpits**?!'

'Oh, it's you two,' a cranky voice said from above.

Angie clumped down the stairs in my body and clothes. My school bag and games bag clumped after her. The Boil was so big and bright today that you could see it from the door without focusing. When she made it to the hall, my mother kissed her on top of the head – and here's a funny thing. I hate being kissed by my mother in front of other people, but when she kissed Angie I felt kind of...jealous. Yes, I know it was my head her lips were decorating with saliva, but I wasn't wearing it at the time, so it wasn't the same, was it?

'See you later,' she said to Angie. 'Have a good day, Musketeers!'

As we sloped down the path, I peered at Angie.

'Ange, why are my eyes so red? What have you been doing to them? Hey, you haven't been...?'

'No, I have not!' she said. 'If you must know, the free extra attachment got stuck in your zip!'

'Ouch,' said Pete.

'Takes a little practice,' I said.

'I don't **want** to practise!' she snarled, and marched off.

We'd almost made it off the estate, Angie walking a few steps in front with my boiled nose in the air, when...

'Oi, you free!'

Pete and I stepped aside to let Atkins through. He scooted on to catch up with Angie.

'Hi, Jig,' I heard him say. She snarled at him too. Eejit peered at the Boil. 'Ya wanna do summin' abaat that, mate. Could turn sceptic.'

Angie didn't thank him for the kind advice. She gripped his scrawny neck, lifted him off the ground, and carried him along while he gasped for breath.

'PUT THAT BOY DOWN, McCUE!' roared a voice like a foghorn.

'I didn't touch him!' I cried, spinning round with my hands up.

Miss Weeks and Mr Rice, our PE teachers, jogged by, him in his stupid red tracksuit, her in her nice green one. Miss Weeks smiled, thinking I was Angie, and fooling around, and even Rice didn't look quite as mean as usual, probably because he was with her.

'If you want to sue him for assault, Atkins,' Rice said, 'we'll gladly be witnesses for the prosecution!'

Angie dropped Eejit and he scampered after the happy joggers, wormed his way between them for protection, and tried to match them jog for jog.

Angie was still ahead of us, so she reached the shopping centre first. We have to go through the shopping centre to get to school. A kid with dreadlocks and a dog leaned out of the doorway of the hairdressers and shoved a magazine in her face.

'*Fat Chance!* Help the homeless! *Fat Chance!*'

'Aw, help yourself!' Angie said, and slapped the magazine out of his hand.

The *Fat Chance* seller shrank back into the doorway. So did the dog.

I felt a worry coming on. Dangerous combination, Angie's temper and my testoblerone. I could see it now. She bursts into the staff-room during break, head-butts every teacher in sight, the Toilet of Doom thing wears off, we get our rightful bodies back, and next morning I'm standing in front of a firing squad in Assembly.

'We have to do something,' I said to Pete. 'We have to make the Toilet of Doom work and get my body back while it's still in one piece.'

'We tried,' he said. 'The door wouldn't open. It might never open again.'

I grabbed him by the shoulders and put Angie's nose against his.

'There must be a way! We have to find it!'

'Go on, Garrett, give 'er a kiss,' said Bryan Ryan, strolling by.

Pete shook me off. 'What are you trying to do to me? This'll be all round school by lunchtime!'

Then he threw himself at Ryan and set about proving he didn't go in for all that soppy stuff. Watching them make mincemeat of one another I suddenly felt very out of things. I'd had it with being a girl.

chapter twelve

You know it's weird, being a girl. The teachers and most of the other kids – even the boys – talk to you differently. Sort of gentler. Doesn't seem natural if you're not used to it. But there was one person who didn't seem to want to talk to me at all. When I walked in the classroom and sat in Angie's seat at the front, Julia Frame turned her back.

'Hey Jools,' I said, 'how's tricks?'

'Huh!' she said.

'Woh,' I said. 'You're not miffed about yesterday, are you? I was kidding, thought you knew that.'

She half turned. 'You were joking?'

''Course I was. I was all set to have a big laugh with you about it when you zonked out of there.'

'You really didn't mean it?'

'Not a word. Not a syllable. Not even a comma.'

It did the job. Too well. She gave a great big sob of relief, threw her arms round me, and squeezed so hard I almost detonated.

'What's all this?'

I looked up. Face-Ache Dakin stood over us. I ducked out of the Frame armlock. 'Practising self-defence, sir,' I said, making some hacking moves at her neck so he'd get the idea.

'Well, in your own time, please. This is a classroom, not a gym.'

He went to his desk, told us to settle down, and started on the register, as usual calling the boys' last names and the girls' first **and** last names, which seems pretty sexist to me. Dakin even calls Milo by his last name in class. Not today, though. Milo wasn't there.

'Julia Frame!' he said, when he got to her.

'Here,' Julia said sulkily. She was half facing the other way again.

'Now what have I done?' I whispered.

'You pushed me off and hacked my neck,' she whispered back.

'I had to,' I said. 'Dakin was—'

'Quiet, you two.'

'Yes, sir. Dakin was here,' I repeated, 'and he's not big on the huggy stuff. If he hadn't loomed over us we could've hugged all day, no prob, but there you go.'

She turned to face me again. She looked like she wanted to believe me.

'Apologise then.'

I sighed. Did I have to go through this every time I opened Angie's mouth?

'OK, but no more bear-hugs in class. I'm sorry I pushed and hacked you. Now can we just sit here and enjoy Registration with our favourite teacher?'

'McCue!' shouted Face-Ache.

I shouted back.

The class stopped talking. Every eye swivelled my way.

'I said McCue, Angela, not Mint.'

'Oh yeah, right, sorry, sir, wasn't paying attention.'

'That's quite an admission for someone in my form.'

'Thanks.'

'McCue!' he said again.

This time I let Angie handle it. Then he said *her* name, which comes right after mine, and I answered again. Not one eyelid batted.

Most days, including Mondays, we don't have any lessons with Face-Ache after Registration, so the second it's over we run for the door. Naturally we make as much noise as we can on the way, and naturally he screams and threatens us with every step – but not today. Today we didn't get a peep out of him.

Outside, our mob headed for the Science Lab.

'Dakin's quiet today,' Angie said on the way.

'I noticed that,' Pete said. 'Spooky, I thought.'

'Almost a different person,' Angie said.

'Like he hired a whole new personality from the New Personality Shop,' said Pete.

'Maybe he's been Toilet of Dooming too,' I said.

'Yes,' said Ange, 'but to switch bods there has to be someone else there, and Milo says they don't get visitors.'

'Maybe they didn't need visitors,' I said. 'Maybe *they* switched.'

'Are you saying it wasn't Dakin the Father taking Registration but Dakin the *Son*?' said Pete.

'Well, it would explain why Milo wasn't in class.'

'Nah. Couldn't happen. If Dakin woke up and discovered he'd turned into Milo overnight he'd have a heart attack.'

'That's it!' I said. 'Face-Ache has a heart attack and Milo leaves him twitching on the floor. "Free at last!" he thinks, sprinting for school in his father's body and clothes.'

Angie shook her head. 'Milo's a young kid in the prime of life and his dad's a dried-up old stick insect. If you were Milo, would you leap at the chance to wear a bag of bones like that?'

'True,' I said. 'Anyway, if Milo took Registration there'd be tell-tale signs. We'd have spotted them.'

'Don't look round,' said Pete. 'I think we're being followed.'

Angie and I looked round. By this time we were the last of our class in the corridor. Last but one. Julia was still there. Trailing after us. After me.

'Think you got yourself a fan,' said Angie.

'Only because she thinks I'm you,' I said.

'No. Because you're being nice to her. Nicer than I ever was.'

It was during morning break that Angie and I had to use the wrong school toilets for the first time. We'd put it off as long as possible – it's a big thing, using the opposite team's toilets – but we couldn't hold it in any longer.

'Go on then,' Angie said, shoving me at the Girls. 'And don't hang about in there.'

'Hang about? This'll be the fastest pee in history.'

I was about to go in when Mr Heathcliff arrived. Heathcliff is the school caretaker, and the most depressing person you ever met. He lives in a cupboard full of brooms and buckets and stuff, and he's always shuffling by muttering things you can't make out. As he shuffled by this time he paused, looked me up and down as if to say he knew all about me and was thinking of selling the story to the tabloids.

'Morning, Mr Heathcliff,' I said.

'Er-*rum!*' he said, which is all he ever seems to say, and shuffled off.

I threw the holy door back and shot in. A girl's gotta do what a girl's gotta do, even when she isn't one. I ran into a cubicle, bolted the door, dropped the fire-damaged underpants, and...well you know the rest. Twenty seconds later I was washing Angie's hands and checking her hair in the mirror.

Now it was Angie's turn. She went to the Boys, followed by us.

'No one comes in,' she said. 'Right?'

Pete and I stood to attention outside – and of course a batch of boys came along right away. One of them was my arch-enemy Bryan Ryan. Only today he didn't know he was my arch-enemy.

'What's up, Minty?' he said when I blocked his way.

'You can't go in there.'

'Why not?'

'Teachers' orders. Flooded. Gotta use the Girls.'

'You're kidding.'

'Would I kid you, Bry-Ry?'

'Well what do the girls use?'

'The Teachers'.'

'So what do the teachers use?'

'The Boys.'

'Oh.'

He and his mates went into the Girls. Pete and I legged it round the corner. We heard screams and yells. Peeked out and saw Ryan and Co shoot out again, ducking lethal toilet rolls.

chapter thirteen

Take it from me, the hardest part about being a girl at school isn't the lessons, it's remembering to sit with your legs together all the time. But even this was nothing compared to Games that Monday afternoon. Things looked like getting kind of tricky before we even left the changing room. I didn't know where to look when the girls started to get into their togs and they thought I was playing the fool when I put my Games knickers on. Games knickers are worn over ordinary knickers. But I wasn't wearing ordinary knickers. I was wearing fire-damaged Y-fronts.

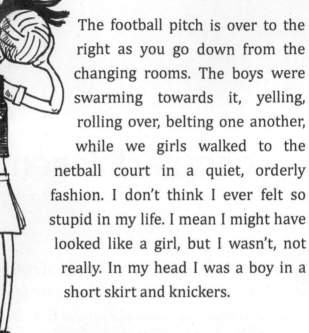

The football pitch is over to the right as you go down from the changing rooms. The boys were swarming towards it, yelling, rolling over, belting one another, while we girls walked to the netball court in a quiet, orderly fashion. I don't think I ever felt so stupid in my life. I mean I might have looked like a girl, but I wasn't, not really. In my head I was a boy in a short skirt and knickers.

The netball court has a high wire fence all round it, like a big cage. Miss Weeks – who was wearing the same natty little green outfit as us – opened the gate and we trooped in. 'Red team that end, blue team that!' Miss said, sticking her arms out like a scarecrow.

'Which am I?' I asked.

'Look at your chest, Angela.'

'Why, what's wrong with it?'

'Your bib, don't be silly.'

'Bib? This thing's called a **bib**?'

I looked at the so-called bib on Angie's chest. It was a red one (bib, not chest). About half the girls wore red bibs, the rest wore blue ones. Some of the red girls were going one way and some of the blues were going the other, while a few of each stayed where they were, in the middle. I thought I'd better stick to the middle too and hope for the best.

Over on the football pitch some of the boys were banging balls about and tripping one another up and Mr Rice was screaming, 'Hegarty, Sprinz, stop fighting!' For the first time ever I wished I was there with them, about to play football.

Something large and shapeless climbed into the corner of my eye. Julia Frame approaching! I was starting to understand what Angie had against her. I ran across the court to get as far away from her as possible...

'What are you doing over there, Angela?' Miss Weeks shouted. 'In position, please!'

'I have a position?' I shouted back.

She threw another arm out. I followed the arm until I came to Rebecca Frazer.

'Hey, Rebecca,' I said. 'What's my position? Must have got sunstroke yesterday. Can't remember things. Like how to play netball.'

She frowned. Rebecca does a lot of frowning when I'm around, and that's when I'm **not** dressed as a girl. She's always telling me to grow up and stuff. Grow up? At my age?

'Sunstroke?' she said. 'It wasn't that sunny yesterday.'

'It wasn't? Well like I said, I don't remember things. Where do I go?'

'Look at your bib.'

I glanced at Angie's chest again. 'Looking.'

'It says "GS". For goal shooter.'

'Cool. And that means...?'

She peered at me suspiciously. 'What are you up to, Angie?'

'Up to? Me? Come on, Beccs, help me out here.'

'You stand near the net. That net. You throw the ball into it.'

'Thanks. Buy you a glass of water some time.'

I sauntered towards my net. While I was walking I heard Rice yelling orders over on the footie pitch.

'Divide yourselves into two teams by your last initial!' he hollered. '"As" to "Ms" this side of the line, "Ns" to "Zs" that side! Come on, move it!'

'What do you mean last initial, sir?'

That was Pete. And suddenly jealousy struck for the second time that day. It should have been me over there annoying Mr Rice.

'What do I mean?!' Rice bawled. 'I mean the first

letter of your last name, boy, what **else** could I mean?!'

'Oh, right.' Pete glanced my way, then said, in a specially loud voice so I wouldn't miss it: 'So if my name was, say, McCue, my initial would be "M", right? It wouldn't be, say, "B" for Big Girl's Blouse?'

I leapt at the fence. 'I'll get you for that, Garrett, you snot-eyed relic!'

Just then I heard a voice in the distance. My voice.

'It's all right, Jig! I mean Angie! I'll do it!'

I dropped off the fence as Angie, in my body and footie gear, put my head down and started towards Pete like a blind bull. Pete saw her coming, spun round, and headed for the edge of the pitch.

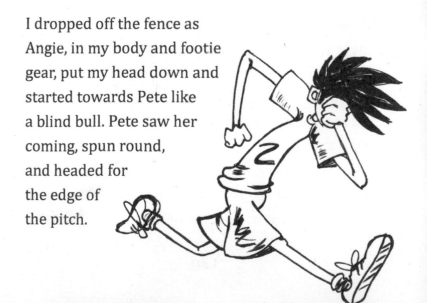

'Garrett, where are you going?!' Rice bawled. 'Set one boot off this pitch and you'll be cleaning the mud off mine for the rest of term!'

Pete swerved. If there's one thing he hates, it's cleaning things. He made a right-angle at the edge of the pitch and started along another side. Not very bright. All Angie had to do now was change direction and take a short cut.

'And what do you think **you're** up to, McCue?!' Rice screamed.

'Gonna duff up Garrett!' Angie yelled.

'Oh no you're not!' he bellowed, going after her. 'There will be no duffing-up in my lesson unless I am the duffer!'

'You are, you are!' hooted several boys at once.

This was followed by a mighty roar as Angie made a flying leap, folded my arms round Pete's legs, and pitched him face-to-face with the worms. Then she jumped up, threw herself astride his back, and grabbed his hair. I don't know what she planned to do next because Rice got there too soon and hauled her off. But he wasn't purple with rage like he usually is when catching a kid pulping another kid.

'That was some tackle, McCue!' he said. 'Could it be that you have hidden talents after all? Let's double check, shall we? Ryan!!!'

'Sir?' said Ryan.

'Run up to my office and fetch a rugger ball!'

'What do you want a rugger ball for, sir? We're playing football.'

'Change of plan! McCue just made the best tackle I've seen here in years! I want to find out if he can do it again! Speed o' light, lad! Everyone else, switch pitch!'

Ryan scowled – he's dotty about football, not rugby – and headed for the changing rooms, while Mr Rice marched towards the rugby pitch. The boys watched him go. When he got there Rice turned, saw that he was alone, and gently asked the boys to please be kind enough to join him.

'GETYERBACKSIDESOVEREREYA USELESSBUNCHALAYABOUTS!'

'All set, Angela?'

I looked round. 'Do you mind if I just watch today, miss? Think I've twisted my ankle.'

I limped bravely round in a little circle to prove it.

'You weren't limping just now.'

'Trying not to, I hate missing netball, but it's so painful.'

'Just do your best. Right, girls, let's get cracking!'

So I played netball for the first time in my life. I picked it up as I went along, and after a while I started to get the hang of it. And guess what? I was good at it. I mean really good. I was a natural. Perhaps it was Angie's body, but even without my jigginess I was so nippy on her feet that the world was a blur. When the ball came my way, all I had to do was reach out and I was holding it. Then all I had to do was stand on tiptoe, make a sharp upward movement, and the ball was dropping out the bottom of the net and my team was cheering and

Miss Weeks was saying, 'Oh well done, Angela, well done, my you *have* come on!'

Every now and then while I was being brilliant at netting balls I glanced across at the rugby field to see how they were getting on. There was one kid who looked like he wanted to make a name for himself. He did a lot of weaving in and out with his head down, the ball pinned to his chest. A lot of elbowing and shouldering anyone who got in the way, and flying through the air and grabbing legs so the owners nose-dived into the daisies. After a while anyone who had any sense headed the other way when he came near. He was terrifying. And who was this warrior of the weird-shaped ball?

Angie.

That's right. Angie. Pretending to be me and shattering my carefully-built-up reputation as an utterly useless sportsman.

chapter fourteen

If you're a boy at Ranting Lane you have to strip off after Games and get in the showers with all the other boys. I hate that, but I would have hated it even more if I'd had to shower with the girls. Fortunately the girls don't have to take showers if they don't want to, so I got dressed with my eyes on the ceiling, wishing girls wouldn't keep coming up to me in towels and patting me on the back, saying things like, 'Hey Angie, didn't know you were such a wiz at netball, can I be in your team next time?' Julia kept looking at me with pride. I gave her the royal wave a couple of times, then cut her out of my will.

I wondered how Angie was getting on. Mr Rice never lets anyone off showers unless they have a fake doctor's note, like Pete, so she would have to shower with the boys. Or so I thought. Should have learnt by now never to underestimate Angie Mint. I waited for her and Pete to come out of the changing room. Pete had mopped most of the dirt off his face, but Angie hadn't bothered. There was mud in my hair, my ears, on my face and neck, under my nails, you name it, there was mud there. Even the Boil was muddy. I asked her how she'd got out of showers.

'Told Rice I had a rash someplace private,' she said.

'That wouldn't stop him throwing a kid in to drown.'

'Ah, but Angie's the flavour of the day,' Pete said. 'You never saw the old Ricebag so pleased. Says she's a real find.'

'Find?'

'As a rugby player.'

I turned away to hide my misery. Because of what Angie had done today, Rice would expect the same sort of performance from me when I got my body back. My only consolation was that next time she donned the little green knickers and bib, Angie would also find herself the star of a sport *she* hates.

Games is the last lesson on Monday so we headed for the gates with everyone else. But then I remembered.

'Whoa! Back up. Detention! Dakin!'

'Curses,' said Pete. 'Forgot that.'

'See ya later,' I said.

'Where are you going?' Angie asked.

'Home. To the wrong house. Garrett and McCue have detentions, not Angie Mint. Better clean yourself up though. Face-Ache won't be too thrilled when you turn up looking like you just took a mud bath.'

She stormed back into school, grinding my teeth. Pete followed. It's the first time I've ever seen him head for detention laughing.

When I reached the estate I found something happening in the street between our houses. Barriers had been put up round a man pickaxing a hole while three others watched. Indoors I went straight up to Pete's room, turned on his PC, called up the Toilet of Life with a beating heart. The door with the notice appeared. It still read 'Engaged'. I clicked about insanely for a while, but it didn't open.

Later, when Pete came in, he had some news.

'Milo's disappeared. Dakin said his bed wasn't slept in last night. He must have gone out after we phoned him and not come back. I've never seen Face-Ache like that. All nervy, not strict at all. Didn't even set us any work, just talked about Milo.'

'What did he say?'

'Dunno, wasn't listening. But he did ask us if he said anything last time we spoke to him.'

'What did you tell him?'

'Nothing. He said if Milo isn't home by teatime he's calling the cops.'

'This isn't good,' I said.

'Oh, I don't know. There could be a house-to-house search. Doors kicked in. Tracker dogs up the stairs. We could be thrown into chairs and blinded by spotlights and everything we say taken down and used against us.' His eyes lit up. 'Hey. If Milo's found in a ditch somewhere, we might even be on the telly!'

I shook my head sadly. 'Garrett, I just don't believe you sometimes.'

'Yeah,' he said, eyes still lit. 'But the *telly*...'

chapter fifteen

after tea – and after I'd washed up (it was Angie's turn on their rotten rota) – me and Pete left the house. The hole was still in the road. The man who'd been digging it was tucking into a pizza he'd just had delivered. The other three were watching him eat now. Must have been trainees.

'Remember,' Pete said as we approached my house, 'you have different parents now.'

Once again my mum opened the door. She didn't look in the best of moods.

'Hi, Peg.' I was getting good at this. 'Jiggy in?'

'In his room. Go on up.'

'Thanks, Mum.'

We went upstairs.

'Don't you Knock?'

Angie said as we barged in.

'Since when do I have to knock on my own door?' I said.

'That door is no longer yours.'

It was then that I realised there was something different about my room.

'Angie. What have you done?'

'I tidied things up.'

'Tidied things up? It's like I was never here.'

'Yes, it's quite an improvement.'

'What are all these cushions doing here? You breeding them or something?'

They were everywhere you looked, about three thousand of them.

'I like cushions,' she said.

'If you like them so much why are there only two in your room? Your real room across the road.'

'We don't have a cushion surplus. Stacks here though. Your mum likes cushions too. Says you and your dad are always taking the mick out of her and her cushions, so she buys them and puts them away for a rainy day.'

'Cushions won't keep the rain off,' said Pete, stretching his arms out and belly-flopping onto a pile of them.

'Apart from the big cushion invasion,' I said, 'what's new around here?'

'Well, your mum's not speaking to your dad,' Angie said.

'That's not new.'

'She's really wound up about him taking Stallone to the vet's behind her back.'

'Why does she have a vet behind her back?' said Pete from the cushion jungle.

'You mean he went through with it?' I said. 'I thought it was just a heat-of-the-moment threat and he'd get over it.'

Angie shook my head. 'He told me everything while hiding from your mum. How he put on these extra-thick lumberjack gloves and snuck up on Stallone while he was eating the jellied pigeon brains he'd bought to distract him. How he put a rope round his neck and dragged him squealing into a cage he'd made specially.'

'So he really had the mad mog done?' I said. 'Poor old Stallone.'

'Not so poor. He broke out of the cage in the waiting room and hasn't been seen since.'

'Like Milo,' said Pete.

'We ought to go and look for him,' I said.

'Who, Milo or Stallone?'

'I meant Stallone, but we could make it a double search.'

'We could,' said Ange. 'Soon as we've checked if the Toilet of Doom's still engaged.'

'It is,' I said. 'I took a look while you were doing my detention.'

'That was then. From what Milo said there's no telling when it'll work next, so we're going to check it again.'

We left the house and started across the road.

'Stallone!' I cried suddenly.

'It's no good shouting for him,' said Angie.

'No, I've just seen him. Look!'

He was sitting under a lamp-post some way along,
one leg in the air while he licked it. It wasn't till we
got within hissing distance that he stopped licking,
dropped the leg, and ran
away on it and three
others.

'Should we go after him?' Angie asked.

'Never catch him,' I said. 'He'll come home when he's
ready. Or not.'

The four workmen were at their hole again, drilling. Pete's room overlooks the street, so the drill was still pretty loud up there even with the window closed. Angie pushed him into his swivel chair and told him to call up the Toilet of Doom. He did. And this time...

'Told you it was worth trying,' she said.

'Click it, Pete, click it!' I said excitedly.

Pete clicked the 'Vacant' sign and the door swung open. And there it was.

The Toilet of Life
A Manx Game

He clicked the little handle on the side, and there was a flushing sound, and the toilet was immediately replaced by the screenful of much smaller toilets and all the little walking people.

'Get flushing!' I commanded.

While Pete did this, Ange and I looked at one another with each other's shining eyes. We were in with a chance of getting our bodies back!

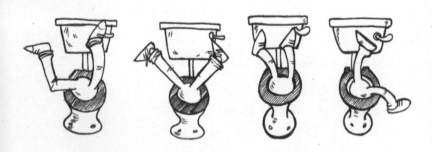

And then all the little people were flushed away, and the screen changed, and we were looking at the Toilet of Life itself, and the immortal words:

Feel that your life has gone down the pan?

Well here's your chance to swap it for a better one.

Just invite someone round who's really got it made and hit 'F for Flush'!

Angie and I slapped hands in the air. At the very instant we slapped hands the drill out in the street stopped. It stopped because the workman and his watchers had drilled through a power cable. All the electricity on our side of the estate went off. Pete's screen went blank. And stayed that way till way past bedtime.

chapter sixteen

first thing in the morning I went to Pete's room and activated his computer. He raised his head from his pillow, asked me what I was doing, I told him to go back to sleep, and he did.

The Toilet of Doom was still vacant. But there was no point going to the next stage because Angie wasn't there. She had to be there when we hit '**F for Flush**' or I might find I'd swapped her body for something even worse, like a cockroach.

We'd arranged to meet for school half an hour earlier that morning. We wanted to see if Milo had returned home. The street was quiet when Pete and I left the house. The electricity vandal and his watchers hadn't arrived yet for another bash at their hole. Angie came out of my house as we reached it. The Boil was starting to fester. Looked like it was getting all set to blow. I put Pete between us.

On the way to Milo's, Angie updated me on life at home. Mum still wasn't talking to Dad because Stallone was still missing.

'She sent your dad out to look for him last night. He was gone for hours. Came back without Stallone but smelling of beer, so she's even less happy with him than before.'

When we got to Pizzle End Road we lurked behind a tree near Milo's and waited for someone to come out. The only one who did was Face-Ache. They never go to school together, so this told us nothing. His walk did though. All stooped and tragic like he was really suffering. Still, we had to make sure. When

Dakin was well on his way we opened the gate and rapped the super-shiny brass knocker for a couple of minutes. The door didn't open.

'Tracker dogs,' said Pete, rubbing his hands. 'Any time now.'

Approaching Mr Mann's bus shelter we saw men in dungarees carrying brand new furniture into the luxury apartment building opposite.

'My dad gets really worked up about that place,' Pete said. 'Gets right up his snout that some people have that sort of money while he only has one car, six ties and a felt tip.'

'Wonder who owns them?' I said.

'My dad,' said Pete.

'The building,' I said.

'No one knows,' said Ange. 'The owner's anonymous.'

'I know that. What I'm saying is, why would someone who owns a block of flats keep it secret?'

'Something happening there,' said Pete.

 Four big teenage boys stood over Mr Mann, who'd just looked up from his paper to see what was in his light. One of the boys was Jolyon Atkins, Eejit Atkins's older brother. We keep out of Jolyon's way. Everyone keeps out of Jolyon's way. He has this barbed-wire tattoo round his neck and the four fingers of his left hand and his right hand are tattooed with H.A.T.E. No L.O.V.E. for Jolyon Atkins.

We crept closer to catch what Jolyon and his gang were saying to Mr Mann. It went something like this:

'You's a tramp, 'at's wot you are.'

'Yer. Why'n't you tramp orf to sum uvver place?'

'Yer. We don' want your kind 'ere.'

'Nah. You're scum. Sod orf.'

'Yer. Or we'll fump ya.'

Mr Mann took his glasses off, smiled, and said, 'Take a seat, lads, sit and chat a while. You're welcome to share my paper. Tell me, what do you make of the latest from the Balkans?'

Jolyon's forehead slumped over his eyes. It was only a little forehead so it didn't have far to go.

'You takin' the proverbial?'

Mr Mann frowned kindly up at him. 'Sorry?

Proverbial what?'

The kindly frown didn't work. Jolyon gripped him by one of the lapels of his old overcoat. The other three leered, made sandpapery noises with their tonsils, all set to enjoy themselves as Jolyon's spare hand folded and drew back.

But then: 'Atkins, you lame-brained twonk, put that tramp down!'

It was my voice.

My real voice.

And it wasn't coming from me.

'Ange,' I whispered confidentially, 'what do you say we keep out of this? I'd kind of like that body

167

to live to see another...'

But she was already stalking towards the bus shelter, where the bundle of bullet-heads stood gaping at her in amazement.

'Wot joo call me, McCue?' Jolyon said.

Angie said. 'And I was being polite.'

'He'll tear her to shreds!' I said to Pete. 'Tear **my body** to shreds!'

'Don't worry,' Pete said, 'you won't feel a thing.'

Now she was standing in front of Jolyon, glaring up at him. She was quite a bit smaller than him, but she didn't seem afraid. While glaring, she unlocked Jolyon's fingers from the tramp's lapel. Mr Mann just sat there looking quietly amused.

'Joo know oo yaw messin' wiv, McCue?' Jolyon said to Angie.

'Course,' she replied. 'I'm messin' wiv a cretin. A twerp. Jolyon Atkins, who has a prune for a brain.'

'No,' I hissed. 'Take it back, Ange, take it back!'

She didn't take it back, and Jolyon's forehead dropped even further. Then he gave her a shove. It was meant to be the first of many shoves, and a lot of other stuff besides. I knew it, Pete knew it, Jolyon's

Merry Men knew it, Mr Mann probably knew it. The only one who didn't seem to was Angie.

'Do that again,' she said, 'and you'll make me angry. You wouldn't like me when I'm angry, Atkins.'

And of course Jolyon did it again. His cronies chuckled. This was gonna be soooo funny. They were still chuckling when a fist dotted Jolyon on the nose. It must have been quite a dot because Jolyon said something like, 'Uh?' and sat down. He stared up at Angie in surprise for a few seconds, then his eyelids drooped and his head slumped forward.

The chuckling of the cronies stopped. Angie turned to them. 'Who's next?'

They held their hands up, shaking their heads.

'Well get him out of here,' Angie said. 'He makes this bus shelter look untidy.'

Jolyon's slack-jawed chums slotted their mitts into his pits and dragged him away, face down.

'Come on, Pete!' I said.

We reached the bus shelter three seconds later, panting for breath.

'You all right, Ange?' I asked. 'It was all so quick, couldn't get here before! Did they hurt you? You want us to go after them and give 'em what for?'

'It's all right, everything's under control,' she said quietly.

And then it all floated through my mind: the not-so-distant day when I'm back in my own body and Jolyon Atkins remembers what happened here today and comes looking for me with a sledgehammer.

I heard Mr Mann's voice in the distance. 'What's your name, son?'

And Angie's reply. 'Jiggy. Jiggy McCue.'

'Well, Jiggy McCue, I'm in your debt. I'd like to give you something for your trouble, a reward of some sort.' Then he spread his arms to take in all his worldly goods. 'I'd *like* to, but as you see...'

'Forget it,' Angie said. 'Glad to be of help.'

'I appreciate that,' said Mr Mann. 'But if there's anything I can ever do for you, all you have to do is ask.'

'Thanks.' She turned to go, but then turned back. 'Wait. There might be something. A friend of ours has gone missing. Milo Dakin, lives just up there.'

'I know Milo,' Mr Mann said. 'Good boy. Often stops for a few words.'

'Yes, well he didn't go home Sunday night and he wasn't at school yesterday, and things haven't been all that great at home for him lately, and I was wondering...well, if you've seen him.'

Mr Mann sucked his lip for a while. Then he said: 'I can tell you something. It's not much, but you must promise not to pass it on to a living soul.'

Angie looked at Pete and me. 'You have our word,' she said.

'Well then, rest assured. Milo is safe and has a roof over his head.'

'Has he told you that?'

Mr Mann looked away. 'Let's just say that one hears things on the street. Now what happened to my paper...?'

His paper had fallen on the ground. I scooped it up and handed it to him.

He gave a bristly smile. 'I'd be lost without my morning paper. Mr Murdoch the newsagent very kindly brings it to me every morning – free of charge.'

'You must know it by heart,' said Pete.

We went on to school.

chapter seventeen

the first thing we saw when we got to school was a notice on a big board in the playground. Standing beside the board was our depressed caretaker, Mr Heathcliff.

'Morning, Mr Heathcliff,' I said.

'Er-***rum***,' he said, and pointed at the notice.

The notice said that everyone must go to the main hall right after Registration. Bit of a puzzle. We only go to the main hall once a week, for Assembly, and Assembly wasn't today.

'Thanks a lot, Mr Heathcliff,' I said as the bell went.

'Er-**rum**.'

'I don't know you bother to talk to that miserable specimen,' Pete said as we went into the building.

'Oh, I enjoy our little chats,' I said.

Not only was Milo not in class again, but his dad wasn't either. Miss Weeks was waiting for us instead.

'Where's Face-Ache, miss?' Pete asked.

'Who?'

'Dakin. Mister. Where?'

'He's about. You'll see him shortly.'

'Oh, good. Hate not to see him every day of my endless school life.'

When she called the register she missed Milo completely. It was as if he'd ceased to exist. After registration, we joined the happy throng in the corridor and set off for the hall. Most of the school was there already, muttering quietly. There was a row of chairs on the stage, with teachers on them looking serious – including Dakin, who looked even tenser than usual.

'Looks worried,' said Angie. 'Maybe he's human after all.'

When everyone was sitting down, Mr Hubbard our headteacher came in with a policeman and a policewoman. He introduced them and they took it in turns, like they'd been rehearsing all night, to tell us about Milo's disappearance and ask us to come forward if we had any information or thoughts as to his whereabouts.

And that was it. We filed out again.

'What do we do?' I said.

'About what?' said Pete.

'Well, Mr Mann seems to know where Milo is. We ought to tell.'

'Can't,' said Angie. 'You gave him our word.'

'Yeah, but this is serious. We could be arrested for withholding stuff.'

'Yes, but if we shop Mr Mann and they interrogate him and he tells everything he knows and they find Milo, they'll ask Milo why he left home, and it might come out that he has a lousy father, which could land Face-Ache in pretty warm water, maybe even lose him his job.'

'That's true,' said Pete. He was halfway to the head's office before we caught him and hauled him back.

First lesson of the day was Geography. Our Geography teacher, Mrs Porterhouse, is very tiny and twice as skinny, with a voice like a bread knife, but she wouldn't be so bad if she didn't keep trying to tell us about people in other countries, like we cared. Today it was Argentina's turn, and the dance they do there. To demonstrate this she took us to the gym.

'Now pay attention, everyone,' she said, slipping a CD into the little machine she'd brought with her. 'The tango is a slow ballroom dance that...' The music started before she was ready. 'Well, watch me.' She started gliding and jerking round the gym like a grasshopper with a wooden leg. 'You see? Looong gliding movements punctuated by **ab-rupt** pauses.'

Pete realised how this was going to work even before I did and grabbed the nearest girl so he wouldn't get stuck with me. Megan Larkin screamed and beat him off. Pete held his hands out.

'Anybody?' he said.

There were no takers, but Porterhouse took charge.

'Jodie, he's all yours.'

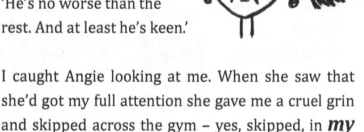

Jodie Walker's face screwed up like an old sweet wrapper. 'Dance with Garrett? Oh *Miss*!'

'He's no worse than the rest. And at least he's keen.'

I caught Angie looking at me. When she saw that she'd got my full attention she gave me a cruel grin and skipped across the gym – yes, skipped, in *my* body! – and grabbed Laura Green by the hand.

Laura tried to yank it back but Angie was too strong for her and pulled her to her, bod to bod, face to face. Then she did a looong glide followed by an abrupt halt. Laura wailed miserably, but Angie kept her grip and did the same thing again, looong glide, abrupt halt, while Mrs Porterhouse clapped.

'Well done, Jiggy, you've really got a feel for the tango!'

I turned to the wall and banged Angie's head slowly against it. In less than a minute she'd killed my cool image stone dead. Boys would be talking about the day Jiggy McCue was praised for dancing the tango till they died laughing of old age.

I hung about as long as possible while partners were being chosen and rejected and forced on other kids, hoping that if I held out to the very end there'd be a boy shortage and I could spend the rest of the lesson sitting cross-legged on the floor doodling in the dust. I should be so lucky. When everyone else was paired off there was just me and one boy left. A boy no girl would dance with even if he was the last one on Earth.

'Come on, you two, don't be shy,' Mrs Porterhouse said. 'Take hold of one another and let's get started.'

I saw Pete cross his legs with delight, and sighed. Well, it had to be done. I gritted Angie's teeth and grabbed Eejit Atkins by the hand. Then I slung an arm round his waist and tested the looong glide.

'Angela, you're the girl,' Porterhouse said. 'It's the male who does the long glides. What you do is drape yourself round his leg and toss your hair.'

I stared at the leg in question. 'You want me to drape myself round *that*?'

'Oh, you can do it. See how well the others are getting on. One or two of them anyway.'

I didn't care how the others were getting on. They didn't have Eejit Atkins's hand on their waist or have to drape themselves over his manky leg. He seemed quite keen, though. As he did a looong glide and twirled me over his leg, he said, 'I never fort I'd be dancin' wiv you, Ange.'

It was then that I realised that Eejit had a thing for Angie. Such a thing did he have that he was grateful for whatever he could get, even a scowl or a thick ear. An idea came to me. A way to get back at Angie for shattering my reputation here and on the sports field.

'Eejit,' I said. 'Ralph. Will you do me a favour?'

'Sure, Ange, wot?'

'Well I really hate the name Angie, so I was thinking, seeing as we're dancing partners now, why don't you call me something else? Something…personal.'

'Pers'nal? Like wot?'

'Special name, just between you and me when there's no one else about. A sort of…pet name.'

'Pet name? You mean like…Fido?'

I bit Angie's tongue to stop it exploding.

'No, Ralph, I do not mean a dog's name, I mean something soft, gentle, like, well…Sweet Lips.'

Even Atkins found this a tad hard to swallow.

'Yoo want *me*…to call *yoo*…Sweet Lips?'

'Keep your voice down, cretin,' I said, 'this is between you and me.'

We did some more looong glides, abrupt halts and leg draping while he thought this over. When he'd got it all straight in his skull he said: 'Ya got yerself a deal, Ange.' He lowered his voice and winked. 'I mean...Sweet Lips.'

'But only when we're alone,' I said. 'If there's anyone else within earshot it's still Angie, right? Remember, or I'll smash your face in.'

'Cool,' he said, shooting a foot out and crippling Martin Skinner for the rest of the day.

Picturing Angie's face when she heard Eejit Atkins call her Sweet Lips for the first time, I danced the rest of the lesson away like a girl possessed. Happiest I'd been since I lost my meat and two veg.

chapter eighteen

The three of us were heading home after another hard day at school. Turning into the shopping centre, we jerked to a simultaneous halt. In the middle of the main square there's this big old tree with a railing round it, and on the lowest branch sat...Stallone.

'What do we do?' I said.

'We talk to him,' Angie said, and marched towards the tree. 'Stallone! Here, boy!'

Stallone glanced at her, and snarled.

She held out a hand. 'It's all right, Stal, no one's gonna hurt you.'

'Eaaaarrrrgh,' growled Stallone.

'I don't get it,' Angie said as we joined her. 'He usually comes to me.'

'He comes to Angie,' I said. 'You're not yourself today. You want a mirror?'

Stallone must have heard me because his ears went up. He picked his way to the end of the branch, dropped off, and ran to me, hissing at Angie as he passed. I stooped to stroke him, but as I touched him a shiver went through him and his back arched. He shot out a claw and—

'Ow! You little monster!'

'No fooling that cat,' said Pete as Stallone became a blur on the far side of the square and I whipped out a hanky and dabbed Angie's hand.

I thought that would be the last we'd see of Stallone that day, and I wouldn't have been sorry, but we saw him again as we were passing the park gates. This time he had company.

'Milo,' Angie breathed as we skidded to a halt.

We peered through the tall black railings. They hadn't seen us.

'First time I ever saw Stallone friendly with a non-female,' I said.

'Kindred spirits,' said Ange. 'Both persecuted waifs. Hey Milo!' she called as we went through the gates.

Milo jumped, and looked our way. So did Stallone. We strolled towards them. For a second neither of them moved, then Stallone hoisted his tail and scooted, like he'd been fired from a catapult. Milo didn't hang about either. He also high-tailed it.

'Ever get the feeling you're not welcome?' I said.

'All the time,' said Pete.

Back on the estate we went to my house first so Angie could change out of my school things. I was feeling kind of nervous. I'd been thinking about the Toilet of Doom all day, on and off. What if the sign on the toilet door said '**Engaged**' again? It might be days before it would let us in for a second flush. Angie had already made me a tango king and a rugby star. I dreaded to think what she might turn me into if she had my body much longer.

When she'd changed we headed across the road. The workmen had gone. So had the hole, which they'd disguised with tarmac of a different shade. Indoors we found Angie's mum in rolled-up dungarees and a fancy headscarf.

'Good day?' she said.

'One for the record books,' I said as we started upstairs.

'Keep out of Pete's room,' she called, coming after us.

'Why?'

'I'm giving it a good going over. Hoovering, dusting, polishing, removing all the sweet and chocolate wrappers from under the bed. In fact generally making it habitable.'

Pete scowled. 'I like it unhabitable.'

We went to Angie's room, where we took turns facing the other way while I changed out of her school togs and Pete changed into jeans and T-shirt. Then we went back to my house and up to my ex-room. I wasn't going to admit it to Angie, but the six million cushions were starting to grow on me. Maybe I'd keep a few of them when I got my room back.

We sat around twiddling our toes for a while, feeling helpless. We needed to get to Pete's computer but couldn't. Eventually Angie rang her mum.

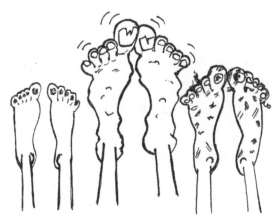

'Pete wants to know how his room's coming along,' she said. She looked at us. 'Slowly, she says.'

Slowly she said and slowly she meant. Every half-hour or so Angie phoned and the answer was always that it wasn't ready yet. Somewhere in all this my mum came home and offered to rustle up chips, beans and sausages. We didn't refuse.

About half eight Angie phoned again, and this time the answer was: 'Almost there, five minutes, God you're a pest, Jiggy.'

We twiddled our bits for five more mins, then recrossed the road. Twenty five minutes later we were finally allowed into Pete's room, which was tidier than it had been since before he moved in and smelt like the inside of a tin of polish.

'It's lost everything!' he wailed, but we didn't give him a chance to wallow in his misery. I turned the computer on and pushed him into his swivel chair.

'Toilet of Doom,' I said. 'Pronto.'

chapter nineteen

The notice on the toilet door still said '**Vacant**'. Good news. The door opened at a single click. Another click activated the toilet handle and brought up the screenful of much smaller toilets. Pete flushed the people in the wink of an eye, and up it came, the thing that had brought this upon Angie and me, the Toilet of Doom itself.

'All yours,' said Pete, vacating the swivel.

Angie pushed me into the chair. 'Get on with it.'

I jumped right out again. 'Oh, no, not me, not again. This time you can get all the stick if it goes wrong.'

She said something uncomplimentary, but took my place at the PC.

'Wait till I'm gone,' Pete said, sprinting to the door. 'Call me when it's over.' He closed the door firmly behind him.

'Ready?' Angie said to me.

'Not really,' I said nervously.

She hit '**F for Flush**'.

And nothing happened.

'Maybe there's a knack,' I said, 'and you don't have it.'

'I'm using your lousy fingers,' she said.

She hit '**F for Flush**' again. Harder.

Still nothing.

'Work, damn you, work!' she said, and hit it again. And again. And again. Nothing happened each time and she got madder and madder.

'Looks like I'm going to have to do it after all,' I said with a kindly smile.

'Over your dead body!' she said, and gave '**F for Flush**' such a belt it's a wonder it didn't turn into a 'Y'.

But it worked. The quivering seat flew up and the blue cloud shot out of the toilet and spread across the inside of the screen, then started seeping into the room and going all sparkly.

'What's taking so long?'
Pete said, looking round the door.

The cloud reached out and hauled him in. The door closed behind him like it had been kicked by an invisible foot.

'Oh, well done, Pete,' I said.

Then all the little sparkly bits started going pop-pop-pop and...

'We forgot about the stink!' Angie cried. 'Why didn't you open the window?'

'Why didn't *you*?' I said.

It was hard to see through all the stinky blue sparkle but we set off towards where the door had been last time we looked – and smacked into Pete also trying to find it. There was a bit of a struggle and quite a lot of unprintable language, but we eventually made it to the landing. As we closed the door, the Toilet of Doom gave a hearty flush.

It was done. For better or worse, it was done.

Halfway downstairs we began to feel dizzy. All three of us. Pete sat down, but Angie and I kept going till we reached the front door. We yanked it open and stood gratefully sucking air.

'Feeling groggy,' she said.

'Me too. But listen, Ange, before we lose it: where do we sleep?'

'Same as last night, case we don't switch back.'

'Yeah, but if we do switch I'll wake up as me in your room and you'll wake up as you in mine. How do we explain that to—?'

'What's going on?' said Oliver Garrett (Pete's dad), looking out of the living room where he was watching TV.

'Just leaving,' Angie said, and tottered off the step.

I shut the door. 'What's with him?' Oliver asked next, meaning the son snoring on the stairs, face jammed between the vertical bars.

'It's been a long day,' I said. 'We had dancing.'

I crawled up to Pete, grabbed him by the collar, and with a superhuman effort bumped him to the top and dragged him into his room. The horrible stink had gone already, and the blue cloud was shrinking back into the screen. I left Pete on the floor and staggered to Angie's room where I flopped onto her bed and slept.

chapter twenty

I woke up feeling different. More myself somehow. My heart thumped. But was it *my* heart? I felt my hair. It was short!

I jumped off the bed. Dropped Angie's jeans. Gripped the band of my fire-damaged Y-fronts. Looked inside. Tears sprang to my eyes.

I was a boy again!

Creeaaak.

Someone outside the door. Oh no! How would I explain this if it was Pete's dad or Angie's mum? I tugged the jeans up and dived under the duvet. Left a tiny gap to peek through as the door opened and the person outside looked in. It wasn't Pete's dad. It wasn't Angie's mum. It wasn't even Pete.

It was me!

I threw back the duvet and sat on the side of the bed, staring at the me in the doorway. What was going on? I'd checked the hardware, knew I wasn't Angie any more, but how could I be in two places at once?

The other me came in, went silently to the dressing table, grabbed a little mirror, brought it to me. I looked into it. The face that stared back wasn't the one I expected...

It was Pete's.

Pete's face? I had Pete Garrett's face? So did that mean...?

The phone on the landing rang. The person who looked like me – who hadn't said a word so far – went out, took the phone off the hook, brought it in.

'Hi, Ange,' he said. 'No, it's Pete. I don't sound like Pete? Now I wonder why that is? Hey wait a minute. It must be something to do with—' he paused, then shouted,

'—THE COLOSSAL BOIL ON THE END OF MY STINKING ROTTEN NOSE!!!'

He clicked the phone off and drop-kicked it across the room.

It rang again almost at once. I scampered to it, picked it up.

'Angie,' I said. 'It's me, Jig.'

'Jig? Are you sure?'

'Not really, no. But you sound like you for a change.'

'I am. What a relief. But what are you two up to?'

'What we're up to is that me and Garrett have switched now.'

'Switched? You mean...'

'Yes. He's now me, and I...' I glared across the room. 'I am **him**.'

'How did that happen?' she asked.

'I can tell you exactly it happened. There was an extra person in the room when the blue cloud did its stuff. A person who shouldn't have been there. A person who left his brain on the landing and came in and

RUINED EVERYTHING!

I threw the phone at Pete. I'm pleased to say that he didn't duck fast enough. What had I done to deserve this? If the T of Doom could only handle one switch at a time, why couldn't it have been me who got his rightful body back? Why couldn't Pete and Angie have switched? At least they could live in their own house!

The phone was still bouncing when it rang again. I snatched it up.

'What!'

'The phone keeps cutting out,' Angie said. 'Must be something wrong with it.'

'At least it's still a _**phone**_!' I snapped.

'Look, we have to get the new show on the road. I need to get out of here before I'm seen. Bring me my school clothes. Clean ones. When you come over Pete can jump into yours and take my place here.'

This time it was she who hung up.

I stormed out, went to Pete's room, climbed into his clothes (all except his underpants) and stormed back. Then I bundled a set of clean clothes for Angie down my shirt.

'Come on, we're going to my house,' I said. 'Don't let yourself be seen. You don't live here today.'

I went down first. Pete crept after me. Downstairs I looked in the kitchen while he slipped out the front door.

'Just going to see Jig for a minute,' I said to Angie's mum. 'Back for breakfast.'

Going after Pete I noticed that he was moving strangely, awkwardly, and realised that unlike Angie he'd got my jigginess.

He reached my house first and rang the plastic bell. Joining him on the step I took a gander at the Boil. It was pretty nasty. Huge and soft, almost transparent, sort of egg-yolky, oozing.

My father answered the door for a change.

'Thought you were upstairs,' he said to Pete.

'New health kick,' Pete snapped. 'Early morning jogs till my eighty-fifth birthday. If I don't keep it up stop my pocket money for life.'

Dad gave my bulging shirt a suspicious look, but let us in. We went up to my room. Angie was waiting for us. It was strange seeing her face on her again. I'd just started to get used to wearing it myself.

She narrowed her eyes at us. 'This better not be your stupid idea of a joke.'

'Joke?' I said. 'Do you see me laughing?'

I opened Pete's shirt and Angie's screwed-up clothes fell out.

'Well thanks a lot,' she said, picking them up and untangling them. But she was all smiles. 'You have no idea how good it is to have your own body back!'

'That's right, rub it in,' I said.

'And I feel so *calm*. Now I know why there's so many wars. It's the testosterone. Men can't help themselves. They have to prove they're the toughest bipeds on the block. Women ought to round them up, put them all on a big island in the middle of nothing and burn the boats.'

'Have you finished?' I said.

'I'm just getting warmed up,' she said.

'Well save it for later. Things to do here.'

'Give me those clothes,' Pete said to Angie.

'Turn the other way then.'

We looked at the wall while she got out of my clothes and put hers on.

'Where you going?' I said when Pete headed for the door with my things under my arm.

'Bathroom, d'you mind?'

When he returned there was something different about him. Something else, I mean.

'Garrett,' I said. 'You evil specimen. You mutant clone of a dung-beetle. You...you...'

I ran out of insults. All I could think of was the state of my beloved face. Stare helplessly at the red and yellow lava streaming from the squashed mini-volcano on my nose. Pete grinned. With my lips, my teeth.

'I've been wanting to burst that thing for days,' he said.

chapter twenty one

angie might have been glad to have her body back, but I kind of missed the calm feeling that came with wearing her carcass. Kind of nice to have all the right attachments back, though, even if they weren't my own.

By lunchtime Pete and I didn't hate each other quite as much, and we went with Angie to our private bench in the Concrete Garden. Over in the playground Mr Dakin was on whistle duty, but he didn't whistle once, just wandered about in these sad little circles while kids beat one another up all round him.

'I feel quite sorry for him,' said Angie. 'Look at him, he's so unhappy.'

'Good,' said Pete.

She sighed. 'Garrett, you have no heart.'

'I do,' he said. 'Jiggy's.'

'We've got to persuade Milo to go back home,' Angie said. 'It's not safe for a kid out there.'

'Have to catch him first,' I said. 'Don't forget, he runs from us.'

'So we run faster. He's got to go home, no question.'

'Ah there you are, McCue, been looking for you everywhere!' boomed a voice so loud and seriously macho that the crisps in our fingers trembled.

'Whatever it is I didn't do it,' I said to Mr Rice.

'Not you, Garrett, McCue. Got some news for you!' he said to Pete. 'You've volunteered for the school rugby team!'

'I didn't know we had a rugby team,' Pete said.

'We didn't! But after Monday, when you showed what you can do, I decided to put one together!'

'When I showed what...? Oh yeah.' Pete grinned at Ange and me. 'Good, wasn't I?'

'Didn't know you had it in you!' said Rice. 'Changing room, tomorrow lunchtime, full kit!'

'Lunchtime?' Pete said. 'No, no. Lunchtime's when lunch gets eaten. That's why it's called lunchtime. I know it's kind of hard to get your head round, sir, but you really have to try.'

'Never mind **lunch**, lad! This could be the making of you! Do well and you could end up representing the nation in the Baghdad Olympics! Lunchtime tomorrow, changing room, or I'll hunt you down like a mangy dog and use your bladder as a lampshade!'

'Thanks a lot, Ange,' I said when he'd gone. 'I always wanted to be Sporty Type of the Year.'

'Sorry, Jig. Got a bit carried away.'

'You should worry,' Pete said to me. 'It's not you who'll be spending tomorrow lunchtime face down in the mud.'

'Oh, yes it is,' I said. 'Because first thing we do when we get home today is flush ourselves back into the right bodies.'

'Not if the "**Engaged**" sign's back we won't.'

'Think positive. This time tomorrow I want you sitting here happily munching and slurping while I'm out there making mud pies and a prat of myself.'

'Cool with me,' said Pete.

Angie managed to upset Julia Frame three times that day, mostly by totally ignoring her when Julia wanted to be chummy. She dumped another fan too, before the day was done. We were heading for the school gates after lessons when Eejit Atkins caught up with us, tugged Angie's sleeve, stood on tiptoe,

and said something in her ear. Angie stopped dead,
staring at Eejit in
disbelief.

'Watch this,' I whispered to Pete.

'**What** did you say?' Angie asked Eejit.

He did a repeat performance in her ear.

And she belted him.

'Do you know what that little slimeball called me?'
she said as Atkins scampered off.

'No, what?' I asked.

It wasn't easy keeping a straight face, even Pete's, and I must have given myself away because her eyes glinted suddenly.

'Did you put him up to that?' she asked.

'Who, me?' I said innocently.

Not innocently enough, though.

'Prepare to die, McCue,' Angie said.

I took a sudden right instead of the usual left out of the gates and hoofed it.

'Another time, Sweet Lips!' I shouted.

'You won't get far on those legs!' she yelled.

She fought her way through the gate scrum and came after me, followed by Pete wondering what Atkins had said. I'd hardly gone a hundred metres before my legs – Pete's legs – started to tire. Angie was right about them. I managed to make it to Downmarket before they started to give way, but then I had to stop. I expected to be pulped when Angie caught up, but by then she'd seen the funny side and just gave me a little clip round Pete's ear.

'Haven't been here for a while,' Pete said, looking around.

Downmarket used to be the town's main street, but since the new shopping centre was built most people go there instead. Some of the Downmarket shops have gone out of business and a whole bunch of them were knocked down to make way for the block of flats for filthy-rich people. The tradesman's entrance of the flats is on the Downmarket side, but most of the windows face the other way so the filthy rich people don't have to look at the rough side of town.

We walked past the bombed-out tobacconist's, the vandalised betting shop, the little old repair shop where the lights never worked.

'**Fat Chance!** Help the homeless! Get your **Fat Chance** here!'

Angie's arm shot out and pinned Pete and me to a rubbish bin.

'Look!'

The **Fat Chance** seller stood outside the boarded-up travel agent's with a magazine bag at his feet. He wasn't like most **Fat Chance** sellers. You don't often see one in a hairy red wig and wraparound sunglasses. Most of them have a dog too. Not him. He had a cat. And the cat was...

Yep. You've got it.

We went into huddled whisper mode.

'Gotta be careful how we handle this,' Angie said.

'Yeah,' we agreed.

'Delicately. With kid gloves.'

'Absolutely.'

We tiptoed from doorway to doorway till we were just one short of our quarry.

'**Fat Chance**, ladies and gentlemen! Help put a roof over someone's head! **Fat Chance! Fat Chance!**'

'Remember,' Angie whispered. 'Delicate. Kid gloves.'

We nodded.

Then we jumped him.

Dragged him into the boarded-up travel agent's doorway.

chapter twenty two

Stallone didn't hang about while we ripped his new chum's wig and glasses off. Milo stared up at us from the ground.

'Jiggy? Pete? Angie?'

'That's us,' I said. 'Just don't ask who's who.'

'Will you get off me, please?'

When he was on his feet, Angie gripped his left wrist and I gripped his right wrist and Pete got down on one knee to grip both of his ankles.

'Why are you holding on to me, Jig?' he asked Pete.

'Don't want you doing another runner,' Angie said.

'I can run if I want. I like running.'

'But why from us? We're your friends.'

'I have stuff to sort out. Need to be on my own.'

'Talk to us, Milo,' I said.

'I'm not saying a word till you let go of me,' Milo said.

We let go of him.

'What are you doing selling **Fat Chance** anyway?' I asked him.

'I have to eat,' he said. 'I get sixty per cent of every copy I sell.'

'Sixty per cent of nothing won't fill you out much. No one buys **Fat Chance**.'

'Some do. I've sold twenty-nine today.'

We all goggled in amazement. Pete got his voice back first.

'You sold twenty-nine copies of *Fat Chance*? You got sixty per cent of twenty-nine *Fat Chances*?'

'One more and I was going to knock off and go for a seafood kebab,' Milo said.

I did a quick run-through of all the things regular loot like that could buy. 'Milo, how does a person become a *Fat Chance* seller?'

'Well,' he said, 'in my case I know the bloke who publishes it.'

'The publisher of *Fat Chance* lives in our town? And you know him?'

'Yes. Yes.'

'Wow. Wow.'

'Don't you have to be sixteen or eighteen or something to sell things on the street?' Angie asked.

'My friend's pretty laid back about stuff like that,' Milo said. 'I had to try and look older, though, in case the law came along.'

'The hairy red wig and wraparound sunglasses?' I said.

'Yeah. Pretty good, eh?'

'Sure had us fooled.'

'So what gave me away?'

'The cat,' Angie said. 'Saw him with you in the park yesterday, remember?'

'Oh yeah, right.' He smiled. 'I keep bumping into him. Some stray, I s'pose. Good cat. Very gentle, very affectionate.'

I glanced at Angie and Pete. My glance said, 'Affectionate? *Stallone?*'

'Tell us why you ran away from home,' Angie said (to Milo).

'Nothing to tell. I've left, that's all.'

'You can't leave home just like that,' I said. 'I mean I think about it all the time, but I don't **do** it. Worse places than home, Milo.'

'Depends on the home.'

'Your dad's really worried,' Angie said.

He perked up a bit at this. 'He is?'

'Going spare,' said Pete happily.

'Yeah?'

'The police are combing the country for you.'

'They are?'

'Sky'll be full of helicopters any time now,' Pete said, looking up.

'Cool.'

'Where are you sleeping?' Angie asked. 'Not in one of these doorways.'

'No, not in a doorway.'

'So where?'

At this Milo came over all sly. 'Somewhere.'

'Well obviously **somewhere,**' Angie said. '***Where*** is what I'm asking.'

'How do I know you won't tell anyone?'

'Milo, it's us,' I said. 'We're on your side.'

He considered this. Then said, 'All right. But you

have to swear you won't tell anyone. I mean ***anyone***, and when I say "tell" that includes writing it down,

signing,

and drawing directions.'

'Ya got a deal.' I looked at the others. 'Right?'

'Right,' said Angie.

'Whatever,' said Pete.

Milo picked up the wig and sunglasses and stuffed them in his magazine bag. He slung the bag over his shoulder.

'It's up here.'

We parted to let him through but crowded him all along the street so he couldn't change his mind and make a break for it.

'Here we are,' he said, stopping suddenly.

'This is the tradesman's entrance of the luxury flats,' Angie said.

Milo smiled and fished a keyring out of his pocket. There were two keys on it. He slotted one of them

in the lock and opened the door. He pushed us inside, then turned a light on and shut the door.

'Where'd you get those keys?' Angie demanded.

'A friend.'

'You're very popular all of a sudden. Who's this one?'

'You don't need to know.'

There wasn't much to see. It was just a sort of hallway with a big plain lift. No luxuries for tradesmen.

Milo thumbed the button to call the lift. The doors sprang back.

'Get in.'

We weren't exactly delirious about this. Our friend and classmate Milo Dakin had keys to the block of flats that only filthy-rich people and tradesmen can enter, and we weren't either of those. Milo punched the top button on a vertical panel.

'You're not sleeping on the roof?' I said as the doors swished shut and the lift shot up like a rocket.

'Just under it.'

In no time the lift was stopping at the top floor and the doors were swishing back. We stepped into a little hallway almost identical to the one at the bottom.

'Here?' Angie said.

'Almost,' said Milo.

He opened a door. On the other side there was another little hallway, a much smarter one, with a couple of nice pictures on the wall and soft lighting, and a luxury carpet so thick it felt like quicksand. There was another lift too, but this one had doors like mirrors. And that was it, apart from one final door. The final door was made of polished wood and on it there were two words.

In films the penthouse is always the apartment right at the top of the building, the best one, the richest one, the one with the best views and all.

'Don't tell us,' said Pete. 'You live in the penthouse.'

We had a good laugh about that. We only stopped laughing when Milo stuck the second key in the door, opened it, and went in.

'What are you standing out there for?' he said.

chapter twenty three

We stepped into the penthouse like three little mice into some big old fat cat's luxury litter tray. The door closed quietly behind us. Everything about the place was quiet. In the first room, the living room, there  was a luxury couch and chairs, a luxury coffee table, luxury curtains and lampshades. We wandered into the other rooms, checked out the three luxury bedrooms, the luxury bathroom, luxury kitchen, luxury fridge magnets. It was a luxurious place.

I went back to the living room ahead of the others. I wanted to see the view from the luxury windows that ran along one side of the room. I've lived in this town all my life but I never had a chance to see it from so high up before. And oh boy. I had no idea it was so beautiful. Even the crummy old Old Town immediately below looked good from there.

I heard Angie's voice, speaking in the luxury distance behind me.

'You can be had up for breaking into rich people's gaffs, Milo.'

'I didn't break in,' he replied. 'You saw the keys.'

'I saw them, but I don't know where you got them.'

'I told you, they belong to a friend of mine. He owns this place.'

'Nobody owns these flats,' I said from the beautiful view. 'They're rented out by this anonymous cove.'

'My friend's the anonymous cove,' Milo said.

'What!'

'He's letting me stay here because this one isn't rented yet.'

'Are you trying to tell us,' Angie said slowly, 'that as well as being all buddy-bud-buds with the publisher of **Fat Chance**, you're pals with the owner of a luxury building for the super-rich?'

'Plus the evil genius who created the Toilet of Life,' said Pete. 'Don't forget him.'

'They're all the same person,' said Milo.

'All the ***same***?' I said, gaping a little.

'How come you know such a person?' said Angie.

Milo shifted from one foot to the other. 'He asked me not talk about him.'

'Milo, listen. Anything you tell us won't leave this room. That's a promise.'

He thought about this. Then sighed.

'All right. But I can't tell you everything. My friend started this games company and it made him rich.

He had half a dozen cars,

couple of fantastic homes,

a stack of people working for him,

and a wife and two kids he almost never saw.'

'Why didn't he see the wife and kids?' Angie asked.

'He was too busy. Not enough hours in the day.'

'Bet the wife didn't like that.'

'She walked out on him and took the
kids. It hit him hard. He sent her
tickets for a no-
expense-spared
holiday in the
Bahamas for
her and the
kids. Thought
that after she'd spent
some time on a beach with
palm trees and hammocks
she'd come back to him and
they'd live happily ever after.'

'And?'

'The plane went down on the way there.'

'Is there anything to eat in this joint?' said Pete, strolling out of the room.

'Went down?' Angie said in horror. 'You mean...?'

'Everyone on board was killed.' Milo sighed. 'He blamed himself. Almost went crazy. Sold the business, cars, houses, got rid of the staff. Vowed never again to care about his own comfort.'

'He owns this building,' Angie said. 'He obviously didn't give everything up if he owns all this.'

'Oh, he doesn't make anything out of this. Hands over every penny he takes in rent to good causes, helps people who need it.'

'Anonymously,' I said.

'Right,' said Milo.

'What I don't understand,' said Angie, 'is why, if your filthy rich pal lets you stay here for nothing, you have to sell **Fat Chance** to make food money.'

'He's providing a bed and shelter but I have to get my own food in,' Milo said. 'It's his only condition. He doesn't believe in free rides.'

Pete bounded back in with the biggest box of chocolates you ever saw.

'Can I open this, Milo?'

'Help yourself,' he said. 'Some woman gave it to me in the street. Very big woman. Said **Fat Chance** made her feel guilty.'

'Probably thought it was a slimming magazine,' I said.

Pete ripped the lid off the box of chocs and got stuck in. I groaned. My poor body!

'What's up, Milo?' I heard Angie say.

Milo had slumped onto the couch.

'Ah, nothing. Well yes. I sort of – stupid I know – miss home.'

'That's not stupid,' Angie said.

'It is in his case,' said Pete, packing my gob with chocolate.

'I mean it's nice enough here,' Milo said. 'I can do anything I like except scribble on the walls, but...you know what? When I moved in the other day I threw my stuff all over the place, and then, next morning...'

Angie sat down next to him. 'You tidied up again.'

He nodded. 'Put it all in alphabetical order.'

'Sounds to me like you don't belong here. Be happier at home.'

'Oh, I wouldn't say **happier**.'

But she'd hit the nail, you could tell.

'Your dad'll be glad to see you. He's gone all quiet since you left. Hasn't handed out a single detention all week and walks around with his head down – like this.'

She got up and did a New Face-Ache impression around the room.

'He walks like that?' Milo said.

'Yeah. It's quite tragic.'

That did it. Milo's heart strings were well and truly twisted, and for the next ten minutes Angie plucked them mercilessly with tales of how sad his rotten father was, how she was sure he was a reformed character and all, until the tears were bouncing off Milo's cheeks like liquid confetti.

After that it was just a matter of time before he was gathering up the carrier bags he'd brought from home and leading the way to the door. 'Oops, almost forgot,' he said, and went back for a thin grey case that stood against a wall. 'My friend's laptop. Been looking after it for him. He asked me to take it to him tomorrow so he can shut down the toilet game.'

'He runs the **Toilet of Doo – Toilet of Life –** from that?' I said.

'Guess so. He doesn't have a high-tech office or anything.'

'And he's gonna shut it down?'

'So he says. It's turned out to be a scientific breakthrough we're not ready for, he tells me. By this time tomorrow the **Toilet of Life** will be no more.'

'No more...' I said faintly.

Well that's it, I thought. I'm stewed. I'm going to be Pete Garrett till the day his heart gives out.

chapter twenty four

When we left the penthouse the ginormous box of chocs went with Pete. He hadn't heard a word Milo said about the **Toilet of Doom** being shut down. Chocolates, chocolates, that's all he was interested in. While he stuffed them one after the other into my mouth, I pulled Angie back a bit.

'I think we should tell him,' I whispered.

'Tell Pete he's a pig?'

'No, Milo about the body-switch. Then he can ask his friend not to shut the T of D down till we've flushed ourselves back.'

'This isn't the time,' she said. 'Look at his little face. He's excited. I bet he hasn't felt this keen to go home since before his mum left. This is an important moment for him. We can't throw a whole new set of spanners in his works.'

'One spanner, that's all I'm asking. And all he has to do is pass it on to his pal.'

'No,' she said firmly. 'We'll flush you and Pete back when we get home and that'll be the end of all this.'

'The "**Engaged**" sign might be back by then.'

'Chance we'll have to take.'

'Funny how you're happy to take chances when it's not you that stands to lose your body forever to someone who has no respect for it,' I said.

Pete was struggling by the time we turned into Pizzle End Road, but he valiantly polished off the last chocolate. 'Whew,' he said, forcing the empty box into an overcrowded litter bin. 'Never thought I'd manage all of 'em.'

'I really wish you hadn't,' I said.

As we reached the gate between Dakin's perfect hedge, Milo had an attack of nerves. 'He could lose it when he sees me on the step,' he said.

'He could,' Angie said. 'But you have to do this, Milo.'

'Yeah. Guess I do.'

He stood up and stuck his chest out. Lifted the catch on the gate. Walked up the path. Banged the shiny knocker.

'Doesn't he have a key?' I asked Angie.

'No. Says his dad plans to give him one, gift-wrapped, when he's thirty.'

We watched through the perfect little holes in the hedge. Saw the door open, super-slow, like it was being opened by a very old lady, or a gerbil. Then there was Face-Ache on the WELCOME, WIPE YOUR FEET mat. But he was so different from the Face-Ache we knew and hated, sort of feeble and lost instead of fierce and tense. His hair was all over the place and his shoulders looked like they could use a coat hanger. The finishing touch, the cardigan and tartan slippers, made you want to call the Samaritans.

'Hi, Dad,' said Milo.

It could have gone either way. Dakin could have immediately snapped up straight and started shouting, bundled Milo inside and told him to vacuum the stairs and ***do a good job***. But instead the sorrow on the old boy's phizog switched to instant happiness, and he grabbed Milo and... hugged him.

Yes, we actually saw Face-Ache Dakin in a full-frontal man-to-boy hug.

'Aaaaah,' said Ange.

'Gets you right there,' I said.

'I feel sick,' said Pete.

Then Dakin hauled Milo inside and the door closed behind them.

'How's that for a happy ending then?' Angie said.

'Hard to beat,' I said. 'Now how about one for me? The one that has to happen tonight if I don't want to be tottering to the post office sixty years from now with a pension book marked "Pete Garrett".

Just then there was a sound to our right. It was like someone puking. We looked towards the sound. It was Pete. Puking.

Into Face-Ache Dakin's perfect hedge.

I was all for going straight up to Pete's room when we got back, but Pete was too green around the gills and slunk off to my house for a lie-down.

'Probably just as well,' Angie pointed out. 'I mean if you switched bodies now it'd be you feeling unwell, not him.'

'True,' I said. 'Yeah, let him suffer. But we have to do it tonight. I do **not** want to wake up in this carcass tomorrow.'

We gave Pete a couple of hours. When he finally tottered over he looked terrible but I called up the **Toilet of Life** anyway. The '**Vacant**' notice was still on the door. I clicked it and the door opened on the toilet with the handle. I clicked the handle, the toilet flushed, and the screenful of much smaller toilets and people took its place. I forced Pete into the swivel chair.

'Get clicking,' I said.

He got clicking, but slower than usual, like every click hurt. Eventually the **Toilet of Life** came up with the banner inviting us to hit **'F for Flush'**.

'Nothing must go wrong this time,' I told Pete. 'When I wake up in the morning I want to be back in my own body and no one else's.'

'You're welcome to it,' he said. 'Your guts are killing me.'

'Might be a good idea to open the window and let the stink out,' Angie said.

'I smell no stink,' I said.

'I mean the one the blue cloud brings.'

She opened the window. 'Neighbourhood Catwatch is off on his rounds,' she said, looking out.

I joined her. Across the road, my father was leaving the house to start his nightly Stallone hunt. He was halfway along the street when a fast sleek shadow caught our eye.

'Talk of the devil,' Angie said.

'Devil cat,' I said.

Stallone, unnoticed by my dad, had jumped onto the garage roof below Pete's window and was staring up at us.

'Stallo-oooo-ne,' Angie called softly. 'Come to Angie. Come to Angie now.'

'Do you two cat-lovers mind if we get this over with?' Pete said. 'I need to lie down again.'

I rejoined him at the computer. 'Yeah, let's do it. Next time I see that face I want it to be in a mirror.'

'Likewise,' he said, and hit '**F for Flush**'.

'Not yet!' cried Angie from the window. 'I'm still here!'

'Oh yeah,' said Pete. 'Sorry.'

But it was too late. The toilet seat had flipped up. Angie squawked.

'You pair of prats! Last thing I want is to be turned into one of you losers again!'

She headed for the door as the blue cloud spread across the screen. I caught a movement by the window she'd just left – Stallone, who'd decided to accept her invitation. Angie hauled the door open as he jumped in and tore after her.

Slam. Thud. Cat skull on wood.

'That's women for you, Stal,' I said. 'Make a fuss of you when it suits them, slam the door on you the moment the toilet seat's up.'

'Here it comes,' Pete said as the blue cloud began seeping out of the screen. He got off his chair and backed away. 'Do you think we should hold hands?'

'Not while this body has a pulse,' I said.

So we stood side by side, waiting for the cloud to cover us and do its stuff. Soon we could hardly see for blue fog, and then the sparkly bits appeared and started going pop-pop-pop, and then...the horrible smell. We palmed our noses and staggered about wondering how long we had to put up with it for it to work. When we couldn't take any more, we groped for the door and lurched downstairs.

Angie was waiting for us in the hall. She opened the front door seconds before we got to it and Pete and I leaned out for a bucket or two of oxygen. Then came the need to sleep. Pete headed across the road yawning my head off and I clawed my way back upstairs and opened his bedroom door. The cloud was already shrinking back into the computer, its work done. I started groggily for the bed and tripped over something: Stallone, who'd passed out on the floor.

I dropped on to the bed. It was done. It was over. A few hours from now I'd be myself again.

Wouldn't I?

chapter twenty five

arly. Very. A voice calling me. Quietly.

'Jig? Pete? Whichever you are, are you awake?'

A hand pinched my shoulder.

I lifted the pillow from
my face and squinted up
through half closed lids,
hoping they were my own.

And saw Angie's face crack
in two.

'It worked!'

'Really? You're not fooling around?'

But I knew she wasn't. I knew my own gorgeous voice when I heard it. I still looked in the mirror Angie handed me, though. I kissed it. Oh, that beautiful burst boil! I was so happy I could even put up with the ache in my guts from all the chocolate Pete had shoved into them.

I was about to get up when I caught a movement on the far side of the bed. I peered over. Saw Pete, curled up on the floor, just waking up.

He was starkers.

'Garrett, what are you doing here?' I said. 'And have you become a nudist overnight? Don't look, Ange.'

Angie raced round and looked. Pete stared up at us from the floor. But then he jerked to his knees and jumped at Angie. Angie tumbled backwards, and before she even hit the carpet Pete was licking her face.

'Pete, you pinhead, what the hell are you...?!'

She shoved him off. Struggled to her feet. But he wasn't finished with her yet. He started winding himself round her legs and...purring.

'Ange,' I said. 'Hate to say this, but I don't think that's Pete.'

'Not Pete?' she said, swiping at him. 'Course it's Pete – being even more of a knucklebrain than usual.'

'Yeah, but look at him. Does Pete normally do that?'

Now he was sprawling on the floor now with his arms and legs in the air, inviting her to tickle him somewhere private. I threw the duvet over him. He seemed to like that. Started tussling with it.

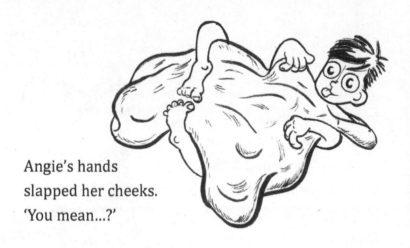

Angie's hands
slapped her cheeks.
'You mean…?'

'Yes,' I said. 'Stallone.'

'But Stallone's a *cat*.'

'Right. And he was in the room with me and Pete when we flushed the T of D last night.'

'He wasn't,' she said.

'Was. He snuck in through the window as you left.'

'But if this is Stallone in Pete's body…'

'Yes,' I said. 'Exactly,' I said. 'What's in my room over the road?'

I went to the window. Across the street my mother had just come out to get the milk in. A small furry creature with four paws and a tail slipped out after her. He hid behind a bush till Mum went back indoors then sauntered to the edge of the pavement, looked left and right, and, when no traffic  came, stood up on his hind legs and crossed the road. With his paws over his dangly bits.

When it was time to leave for school the three of us that were in human form detoured over Milo's way hoping to bump into him and see how things were at home. I felt fantastic. Not only did I finally have my body back, but I was so jiggy I could hardly walk in a straight line.

We were almost at Milo's when we saw him and his dad closing their gate and setting off for school together. Face-Ache's hand rested lightly on Milo's shoulder, and every now and then as they walked Milo looked up at him and...they smiled at one another.

'I never saw Face-Ache so happy,' said Angie.

'It won't do,' I said. 'You can't have someone called Face-Ache being happy.'

Following them at a distance, I noticed that as well as his school bag Milo carried a laptop-shaped carrier bag.

'Why would he be taking the anonymous friend's laptop to school?' I wondered.

'Maybe the anonymous friend's a teacher,' said Ange.

'A teacher? At Ranting Lane? Get real. He might not want people to know who he is, but—'

'Hey, what if it's Mr Rice?'

I laughed. The thought of the Rice Krispie being a secret Good Person who only wanted to help people...per-Rice-less!

As Milo and his old fella drew near Mr Mann's bus shelter someone shuffled past us: a downtrodden, sorrowful soul I'd never seen out of school before.

I stopped. Stared. Suddenly everything fell into place.

'What's up?' said Ange, also stopping.

'I know who it is,' I said, and pointed at the downtrodden, sorrowful figure trudging miserably ahead of us.

'Heathcliff? You can't be serious. I mean he's so...'

'Anonymous? Right. Mr Heathcliff is the most anonymous person in the local universe. He lives in a broom cupboard without any comforts or luxuries except a little telly and three thousand dusters. What a cover! Wouldn't occur to anyone for a *minute* that our humble, depressed school caretaker could also be someone who builds luxury apartments, publishes a magazine for the homeless, and creates dangerous interactive computer games. It's so *obvious* once you think of it!'

'You know,' Angie said thoughtfully, 'you might just be right.'

'I *know* I am. Heathcliff's our man or my name's not Jiggy McCue.'

We started walking again so as to keep Heathcliff, Milo and Face-Ache in sight. Heathcliff surprised us a bit by suddenly shuffling into the road, but we decided he must be going to the filthy-rich apartment block.

'Wants to check everything's in good luxury running order,' I said.

He reached the opposite
pavement just as Milo
and Face-Ache drew
level with Mr Mann's
bus shelter on our
side. Milo grinned
at Mr Mann and
then, without his
father seeing,
slipped him
the laptop. I
glanced across
the road. Heathcliff had
shuffled past the block of flats and gone into
the newsagent's.

'What did you say your name was?' Angie said.

While I struggled to come to terms with this
unexpected twist, a man stepped out of the block of
flats and crossed the road. It was the official-looking
type we'd seen here before. He headed for the bus
shelter and spoke to Mr Mann.

'Let's give them a listen,' Angie said.

The three of us scooted round the back of the bus shelter, where Angie and I pressed our ears to the wood and the third Musketeer rolled into a ball and licked the front of his school trousers.

'Cheque for you to sign,' we heard the official-looking type say. 'The donation to Kids in Need.'

'It only says fifty thousand,' Mr Mann said. 'Wallace, I told you to make it out for twice that.'

'I'm supposed to be looking after your financial affairs,' the Wallace geezer replied. 'I'm trying to stop you bankrupting yourself.'

'Let me worry about that. Tear this up and make out another – for a hundred grand.'

Wallace sighed disapprovingly. 'Well, you're the boss.'

'Yes,' said Mr Mann. 'Remember that please. What's the latest on the flats?'

'Just three still to be let – not counting the penthouse.'

'You can put the penthouse back on the market. My friend doesn't need it any more. Oh, and there's a **Fat Chance** vacancy. Scout around for someone who needs some money and is prepared to graft for it.'

'Yes, sir.'

The man in the suit walked off and me and Ange headed for the other side of the bus shelter. But then she said, 'Oh wait, we're one short,' and dashed back for the third Musketeer, who was sitting on the ground with one leg in the air, licking the inside of it.

'Ah, Jiggy McCue, good morning!' cried a hearty voice.

I turned. Mr Mann was waving at me from his shelter.

'Morning, Mr Mann.'

'Thanks again for what you did the other day!'

'Any time,' I said as the other two joined me.

Angie glared at me. 'Now I ask you, is that right? Is that just? I do someone a really heroic good turn and you get the credit.'

'That's life, Ange,' I chuckled.

We turned a corner. The school was in sight. So were Jolyon Atkins and his bonehead cronies. Spread out across the pavement waiting for us.

'Hiya, McCue,' said Jolyon – and this time he wasn't talking to Angie.

My knees did a sudden magic trick. They turned from knees into jelly.

'Care to do another heroic good turn?' I asked Ange.

'I haven't got enough testosterone now to fluff up a cushion,' she said. 'Better take what's coming to you.'

'But it should be coming to you, not me.'

'That's life, Jig,' she chuckled.

I turned. I ran. So did Angie. So did the third Musketeer, the recycled one. When at last we skidded to a heavy-breathing halt the school was once again in sight, but from a different direction and minus

Jolyon Atkins. The jelly between my ankles and personal places became knees again.

'So,' Angie said. 'All's well that ends well.'

'For two of us anyway,' I said, thinking of Pete, furry Pete, curled up in Stallone's basket back at my house. My mother had been so delighted to see him (or who she thought he was) that she'd taken the day off work to wait on him hand and foot. Pete had never been treated so well. Seemed to quite like the food that went with the job too.

'Fair average, two out of three,' Angie said.

'Yeah. Could be worse.'

I threw my arm out. My very own wonderful right arm, and pointed my own wonderful finger at the road ahead.

'Onward, Musketeers. To school!'

'One for all...' said Angie.

'And all for lunch!' said I.

'Reowl,' said the third Musketeer, and jumped up a tree after a bird.

THE END